EVIDENCE POOL

Murder detectives face a tricky case

IAN ROBINSON

Published by The Book Folks

London, 2023

© Ian Robinson

This book is a work of fiction. Names, characters, businesses, organizations, places and events are either the product of the author's imagination or are used fictitiously. Any resemblance to actual persons, living or dead, events or locales is entirely coincidental. The spelling is British English.

All rights reserved. No part of this publication may be reproduced, stored in retrieval system, copied in any form or by any means, electronic, mechanical, photocopying, recording or otherwise transmitted without written permission from the publisher.

ISBN 978-1-80462-093-9

www.thebookfolks.com

Evidence Pool is the fourth standalone novel in the DI Pippa Nash and DS Nick Moretti mystery series. Details about the other books can be found at the back of this one.

CHAPTER ONE

Alex Petrov's tongue probed his inner cheeks and recoiled as the acidic taste registered with his brain. He'd drunk a significant volume of alcohol the night before, above and beyond his strict rule of consumption for a weekday. He'd broken his self-imposed limit as a reward for securing a major business deal for his government, as well as a side hustle for his own real estate company. He'd stepped down from running his lucrative property empire, handing the reins to another family member, but he liked to keep an eye on his legacy, even if that meant the boundaries between official state business and his own became blurred.

He served his country in the role of advisor. The advisory role was as broad as it was all-consuming but afforded him certain privileges of state whenever he visited other countries. His desire to celebrate had overcome his resolve to treat his body as a temple. His latest private investment would ensure that, from now on, he and his staff team would be accommodated, securely, whenever he was in the UK. It would be a luxury not having to rent anymore.

The dawn of a new day bloomed. For Petrov, every day he was alive meant another twenty-four hours to make money and serve his country. He despised leisure unless it was in the pursuit of fitness.

For now, he was still renting a property when in London. Dappled light crept through the edges of a crushed velvet drape fitted to the master suite. This was no penthouse in Battersea. This rental was a sprawling Georgian mansion situated in one of London's most expensive streets, The Bishops Avenue, N2. The Avenue, as it was known to those who resided there, ran downhill, north to south, from the edge of Hampstead Heath. Known also as Billionaires' Row, its reputation surpassed that of Buckingham Palace. If you owned one of the sixty-six properties that lined the vast expanse of road, you could dispense with having to explain that you were wealthy.

Petrov hadn't bought on this street. He was no fool. He was careful with his own wealth. Most of the properties here remained empty, many were derelict. He'd chosen to stay at Heath Hall, as it had met his needs on numerous occasions when he'd visited the UK on private and state business. It happened to be vacant during the dates he required. Petrov enjoyed the luxuries it provided: indoor and outdoor pools, a cellar stocked with over six hundred wines from the best vineyards on the planet. The bath in the master bedroom was carved from a single block of marble. The same room also housed a steel-walled dressing area that doubled as a panic room should it be required. A suite rather than a single room. The state baulked at paying, but he was happy to pick up the £35,000 per week rental, essential staff included.

Petrov also enjoyed strolling among the two and a half acres of manicured grounds the house sat within. It was a space he could be alone in. As much as anyone with his wealth could, when surrounded by a small team of bodyguards. His close protection team consisted of a contingent of ex-Spetsnaz special forces soldiers, all of whom operated on a twelve-hour shift system. Two on, two off. The rest of his security detail he outsourced through the agency who managed the property. The house was gated. A dog patrol provided additional security that ensured those staying within the walls of the estate were afforded the highest safety measures on the street. Attention to security was high-end, spanning both electronic and human surveillance.

In the exclusive members' brochure, Heath Hall was described as a safe and secure environment in which to retreat while staying in London. An oasis of calm providing the ultimate luxury city escape. A daily sweep of the property was also included. Not with a dustpan and brush, although that took place at regular intervals – not that any resident would be aware – but with a device that would detect listening probes. The gardens and grounds were searched using the keen nose of a bomb-detection dog. All part of the unobtrusive service. As a client, you'd never be aware of the levels of protection being undertaken. They all operated in the background to ensure the stay was hassle-free and, above all, safe.

Petrov rubbed his eyes, and allowed his vision to adjust to stare at the ornate ceiling. He'd told himself he would hit the pool and swim for a hundred lengths no matter how rough he felt. Despite the hour – 5 a.m. – he decided he would continue as promised. Rather than use weights, he'd swim and use the stationary bike.

He'd dismissed his close protection team once they were inside Heath Hall. They'd been exemplary while he was at a London restaurant following a meeting at the Russian embassy. He felt secure within the grounds of the property. House staff managed his welfare while his pod of four personnel grabbed some well-needed rest.

Petrov sat up and stretched. He got out of the ridiculously vast bed, put on his trunks and a soft towelling robe with matching open-heeled slippers.

At home he swam outdoors in all seasons. The ice he saw as his friend. The cold tempered the soul, and hardened the mind and body against stress. Today, he would remain inside. Leaving his bedroom, he descended the staircase. Concealed lights illuminated his way. With every step, sensors in the walls blinked into life activating internal floor lights that, subtly, illuminated his path like an airport runway. His slippers masked the sound of his heavy footfall against the marble of the sweeping stairs. Below, the soothing notes of falling water emanated. All courtesy of an indoor fountain that gently cascaded water from the mouth of a bronze dolphin presented as leaping from the carp-filled pool below. He paused in the foyer and investigated the pool. Taking a pinch of koi food from a bronze bowl, he crumbled the flakes between his thumb and index finger and watched as the water erupted in a mass of suckling fish.

Strolling towards the door to the swimming pool's changing room, he entered and stood next to a carved-stone sink adorned with gold taps.

He stared into a mirror framed in the same carat gold. He noted fine lines at the creases of his eyes. He didn't feel his forty years. He felt more like thirty, certainly in body, if not mind. He wagged his index finger at his reflection. 'You will be punished for your overindulgence last night, my friend,' he admonished himself. 'You will leave the pool hating the very sight of the water. Every trace of alcohol will be evaporated through sweat and exertion. It is the only way to learn about poisoning yourself in such a way.'

Stretching his neck, he smoothed back his dark shoulder-length hair. He pushed through the door into the main pool area. Dawn light stretched across the room thanks to the skylight windows of a vaulted atrium that towered above the surface of the water. The penchant for marble was evident throughout the room. Petrov paused. He was standing near a lounger at the pool edge in preparation to dispense with his robe and slippers. Despite the temperature-controlled atmosphere, his body flushed with cold. The expected blue hue of the water was tainted by an unwelcome patch of red.

The assault on his eyes wasn't blood, however. The mass of colour was the flame-red locks of hair that floated upon the surface of the still water. Petrov staggered back into the frame of the lounger. His heart pounded against the wall of his chest. He opened his mouth to yell, but his efforts were futile.

He wasn't a doctor and had never undertaken any formal medical training, but he instinctively knew the woman was dead. Her hands were splayed palms down, out to her side. Her face dipped beneath the surface of the water. There were no air bubbles. His eyes averted the body for a moment to focus on a red button upon the wall next to him.

He moved around the frame of the lounger and over to the wall where he slammed his palm against the alarm button. There was no raucous siren. It was a silent alert that matched the eerie air he and the woman inhabited. He flopped down onto the lounger and leaned forwards as his breathing became shallow.

The ghostly tranquillity was soon shattered by the arrival of pounding feet as two of his close protection officers burst into the room. On discovering Petrov, both men wasted no time. They scooped him up under the armpits, dragging him out of the pool area.

Petrov looked down his body and back at the water. His eyes caught the unmistakable glint of gold. Gold caught in the water thanks to the outside light that filtered in from above to rest upon the lifeless body of the woman. The glitter was coming from a buckle attached to a belt. A buckle Petrov immediately recognised as his, and the leather it was attached to trailed down the woman's back from her neck.

CHAPTER TWO

DI Pippa Nash didn't want another murder to investigate. Her team had picked up the last three investigations, which had kept them all gainfully employed. The message on her work mobile to call the contact desk suggested that she was out of luck.

She'd missed the call because of an early morning run. Running was a space of her own and she'd left her work phone on the kitchen table at home. Stepping out of a cold shower, she cursed herself for not arranging her boiler repair sooner and leaving it to another outstanding task on her personal to-do list. A list she simply didn't have any time to conquer. She towelled off her hair before shaking it loose. Despite her love of fitness, she desired a cigarette. She'd given up the weed ten years ago, but every now and then, especially at times of stress, she'd experience a desire to spark up. She ignored her cravings and sat at her small kitchen table. She didn't need a dining table for entertaining, just one large enough to accommodate her and maybe one other. It fit well within her compact top-floor flat.

Home was a conversion within a Victorian house. Upon the table sat a stack of decision logs and alongside those her grab bag, complete with all she'd need for a crime scene as the Investigating Officer. She took a decision log from the pile. Opening it to a new page she snapped the spine and laid it down. Her phone glowed 5:30 a.m. Her team were what was known as "in the frame" for the next job. That next job always being a suspicious death. The fact it was neither the end of night shift nor the start of early turn didn't negate her duty. She made the call to the contact desk, noted the details, and phoned her DS, Nick Moretti.

'Nick, be ready at 6 a.m. We've a new case,' she said, pressing the end button on her phone. She'd have enough time to get dressed, collect her scene bag, and then Moretti – whom she was confident would pick up the message and be ready as requested.

* * *

Nash pulled into The Bishops Avenue just as the hazy dawn sun rose in majesty above the roof line of the immense villa that faced her. Shadows from plane trees stretched across the road, a strip of tarmac wide enough to accommodate parked cars while ensuring traveling vehicles continued unhindered. Not that anyone, other than builders' vans, used the road as a car park. Two marked police vehicles were parked outside a mansion house and she pulled in behind them and killed the engine.

Nash and Moretti stepped out to face a set of metal-barred gates that stretched across the driveway to Heath Hall and were of a height that would be daunting to vault. Roadside, a uniformed constable stood alongside a police inspector who was remonstrating with a burly-looking man dressed in a black suit. A trail of clear bunched cable led from the man's neck into an earpiece. The sentry's uniform was finished off with a pair of dark shades, the frames of which were in symmetry with his jawline.

Nash approached the gate and the uniform inspector turned in her direction.

'DI Nash, Homicide Command, why aren't you inside? I was told my scene was in a swimming pool,' she said.

The inspector took off his hat running his hand across his shaved head. He was in his late twenties and, to Nash, appeared way out of his depth.

'Can I have a word away from the gate?' he said.

Nash nodded, leaving Moretti with the PC.

Once they were a reasonable distance from the gatekeeper so they wouldn't be overheard, Nash spoke. 'Well?'

The inspector placed his hat back on and adjusted the peak so his eyes were visible.

'I've done all I can to gain access, but the current occupier is adamant he won't open the gates until the person in charge arrives. They wouldn't accept it was me. The uniform, I guess.'

Nash made no comment. 'Who lives here?' she said, her decision log open, pen hovering over a page.

'It's rented by Alex Petrov. He uses an agency in London. The call to police was made from inside the house. The caller said there was a body in the pool, and they requested police attendance, that was it. I've not had the chance to see the body and have no idea of the circumstances. I was about to escalate the matter to the point of forcing entry when you arrived,' he said.

Nash looked at the gate then back at the inspector.

'What were you thinking of using? A tank?' she said, making a note of what she'd been told. The contact desk had explained they hadn't any information about the body, but the caller was saying they were phoning from inside the premises and the body was in the indoor pool. It was marked up on the system as suspicious unless assessed otherwise. Nash left the inspector and returned to Moretti.

'Right, let's see what we have then,' she said. She pulled her warrant card away from her body by the lanyard and held it by the gap in the bars to the gate.

The sentry leaned forwards and lowered his shades down his nose to read her ID. His eyes scanned left to right. Nash judged that the sentry had been given enough time.

'Open this gate before I have it taken off. I'm sure your boss wouldn't be happy at a hefty repair bill,' she said, lowering her warrant card.

'You are the senior officer, yes?' he said. Nash noted English wasn't his first language by the intonation of his voice, but he spoke clearly, and she felt he had a good grasp of English. Enough to understand that he was obstructing her investigation.

Nash sighed. 'I'm not passing through if that's what you're asking. Like you, I have a job to do. Step aside and let me and my team get on with it,' she said.

The sentry stepped back and spoke into a lapel mic. Nash noted the change in language – Russian. There was a pause, before the guard replied in the same language. The gate began to withdraw to the sides on a track mechanism. Nash and Moretti stepped over the threshold onto a driveway that led to a turning circle before the main entrance to the property – two rotund stone pillars supporting an impressive, pitched roof that sheltered imposing double doors of hand-carved oak.

'Keep that gate open,' Nash said to the sentry, as she and Moretti walked towards the mansion.

The sentry stepped onto an imaginary line of demarcation between property and street, hands crossed at the navel. The gate remained open.

Nash draped her scene bag across her shoulder, the black canvas obscuring her back. The door to the mansion opened as they approached. Nash made a mental note that there were covert cameras. Cameras whose hard drives could contain vital information that would assist her investigation. Security was tight. Something she hoped to exploit as part of her inquiry.

Another suited and booted male framed the doorway to the property. He could have been mistaken for the same man outside, such was the uniformity of build and style of clothing. He held out a hand, not in greeting. His palm faced both detectives.

Nash paused before looking up at the man. 'I'm not usually brusque in my manner when stepping into someone's property; however, I can tell you this, this reception is beginning to piss me off. Either move or accept me barging through. Either choice is good for me,' she said, stepping forwards.

The guard produced a metal-detecting wand from behind his mountain of a back, quickly scanning Nash who swatted the wand away like a petulant fly. The guard shrugged. She looked to Moretti and shook her head before walking in. Moretti didn't suffer the same treatment. Once inside neither detective could believe what they were seeing.

Floor-to-ceiling marble surrounded them. The starkness of the stone felt cold in contrast to the heat of the home. It was like they were visiting a mausoleum. There was nothing soft about it, except for a circular indoor pond. A fountain of water switched colour as it danced in the air from a dolphin's mouth. Wherever they looked it appeared ordered, controlled almost. A sweeping marble staircase towered before them, and Nash let her eyes lead her away to a first-floor landing that parted either side of where she and Moretti were standing.

A light cough from behind interrupted her viewing. Nash turned to see a woman, in her late forties and impeccably dressed. The shock of seeing the immaculately turned-out woman caused Nash to run her hands down her wrinkled suit jacket. The woman blinked.

'Good morning, Detective Inspector, my name's Fiona Middleton. I'm the maître d' at Heath Hall. I've been instructed by Mr Petrov, the current occupier, to show you the utmost consideration while you are here. If there's anything I can do, you only must ask,' she said, with a light dip of her head.

'Well, that's very good of you, Ms Middleton, I'd very much like to do my job unobstructed by the Men in Black. Now, where's Mr Petrov? Where is my scene? Do we know the person in the pool? Not necessarily in that order,' Nash said with a hint of sarcasm.

Middleton raised her eyebrows.

'On Mr Petrov's instructions, I haven't been in there. Mr Petrov requested a guard be placed on the only entrance and exit to the pool area until police arrival. No one has been in there since Mr Petrov discovered the person this morning,' she said, without a hint of distress.

Nash rubbed the bridge of her nose. 'Where is Mr Petrov?' Nash asked.

'In the security suite, or panic room, as it is also known,' Middleton replied, her demeanour suggesting it was a perfectly acceptable place for him to be at this time.

Nash's eyes widened. 'Sorry, are you implying he was having some kind of nervous attack and a lie-down?' she said.

Middleton maintained her professional aura. 'Mr Petrov is in a secure space. There is a suite in the house utilised in the event of a security breach and Mr Petrov's security team felt he may be at risk of significant harm, so he was placed there,' Middleton said.

'A security risk? I very much doubt that, not with the security here. My DS will be taken to see the pool area. I will need to see Mr Petrov once we've assessed the scene. I'll require a list of all staff that have been present since Mr Petrov's arrival. No one is to enter or leave the building unless they are police or police staff, is that clear?' Nash said.

'As you wish,' Middleton said. 'However, you won't be able to see Mr Petrov in person. I have taken the liberty of setting up a room for your use though.'

Nash shot Moretti a glance before returning her attention to Middleton. Middleton remained firm, her feet hips-width apart. She oozed control from every pore. Nash didn't like any of this. She'd been called to attend a crime scene. A scene that had been initially assessed, over the phone, as suspicious. She represented the Metropolitan Police, on behalf of the King. She had no strong affiliations to either party, but Middleton's attitude riled her.

'Mr Petrov will present himself to me, in person. I cannot make that clearer. He's the individual who discovered the body in a swimming pool of a house he resides in. Do I need to spell out what that means in terms of speaking to police?' Nash said.

'I don't think you understand, Inspector…'

'I understand he's in a secure area, but he can venture from there now. The building has better security than New Scotland Yard. He's perfectly safe,' Nash said.

Middleton's eyes dipped to the floor. The tip of her tongue probed the corner of her lips.

'Detective Inspector, Mr Petrov has every right to remain where he is. He will not be coming out of the suite. He has agreed to communicate with you via video link until such a time that he deems his safety can be assured. That is his prerogative,' Middleton said.

Nash nestled her elbow in the palm of her hand as she rubbed her forehead with thumb and index finger. The incredulity of the rich astonished her. How they could deem themselves above the law because of wealth. She had done her best to remain restrained, but this was a step too far.

'Look, you either tell Mr Petrov to get his arse down here or I'll have him arrested for obstructing police and carted off to a cell,' Nash said.

Moretti shuffled his feet to a stance that would help if things progressed to a physical interaction.

'I wouldn't advise that course of action, Inspector,' Middleton said.

'Oh, you're a lawyer as well as head of staff, are you?' Nash said.

'Not at all. I do like to provide an impartial service though. In the interests of your investigation, I think you should be aware that Mr Petrov has chosen to exercise his constitutional right to diplomatic immunity. I'm sure you understand the implications of that aspect of the law, Detective Inspector.'

Nash swallowed. Game set and match to Middleton. But Nash wasn't defeated. She knew that diplomatic immunity wasn't the get-out-of-jail-free card it was often understood to be. She hoped his claim wouldn't stand up to scrutiny, although she was aware she was clutching at straws. Efficiency, it seemed, was everything within the impenetrable walls of Heath Hall.

CHAPTER THREE

Nash and Moretti crouched at the edge of the swimming pool observing the apparently lifeless body of a woman whose flame-red hair fanned, suspended, across her sodden tailored suit. Strands flared out at the edges of her head. Nash could tell the suit was handmade by the way the cloth remained in place against the victim's skin despite the watery setting. No billowing fabric. Every nip and tuck of fabric was where it should be.

Nash started her visual examination, as she always did, at the head. From there, she methodically worked her eyes down the woman's body. If the victim had been on land, she'd have done the same. Every contact leaves a trace. Any of her own DNA or a single fibre from her clothing that made its way upon the victim could waste hours of valuable work for a forensic scientist. This is why barrier clothing, despite being a restrictive garment to work in, is an essential tool in an investigation.

Nash noted that the rear of the victim's head had no obvious wounds from what she could see. Her hair was thick and covered her skull well. Nash surmised it was professionally straightened, too, by the way it sat on the water and clung to rest midway down her back. There was no blood present in the water. A crescent-shaped wooden hair grip hung loose against the back of her head. The strands of hair floated upon the surface like tentacles. Occasionally, the natural light hit it, accentuating the flame-red colour that ran throughout each strand. Nash noted a belt. It was significant as it wasn't where she'd expect to see one.

The belt was dark brown. The colour, she surmised, could be due to the water or the tan of the leather. It was secured around the victim's neck, with the buckle visible at her back. From Nash's position, it was hard to tell how it had been put on. The victim's shoulders were broad. Not overly muscular, but certainly defined. The suit jacket fitted perfectly. Nash had seen a similar V shape on Olympic swimmers. If she was correct, the victim would have been able to get out of the pool if she were alive when she entered it. The belt trailed against the dark suit jacket. The victim wore a matching set of suit trousers with black, heeled shoes.

Nash glanced up to rest her concentration. The ceiling was structured into a dome. A gaudy-looking fresco of angels looked down upon the water. Panels of heat-reflecting glass acted as a wall until they hit the main supporting structure that provided privacy from outside eyes. There were no obvious ligature points. This was no suicide by hanging. The way the belt lay suggested to Nash that it was looped over the head to rest at the neck.

It could have been used as a ligature and pulled from behind, causing suffocation. No easy task. Anyone would have put up a struggle. Judging from the clinical appearance of the pool area, there hadn't been one. Clinical, in that everything was where it should be aside from the body. Middleton had said Petrov had discovered the woman's body before being removed by his security team to the panic room. The pool area had been secured on his instructions. Could they have been told to tidy up?

'What's your thoughts?' she said to Moretti, conscious he'd been quiet since their arrival.

'My initial thoughts are where's the nearest cafe. The posh don't do fry-ups and I'm starving,' he said.

Despite the face mask she could tell by his eyes he was joking. Gallows humour when faced with the macabre. It helped calm the mind at times, preparing it to focus on the realities that couldn't be avoided.

'Sorry. It doesn't look like suicide,' he said.

'Why do you say that?' Nash said.

'Well, she's in the centre of the pool and unless there's a wave machine that's been turned off, I'd suggest she was pushed, or thrown, when dead or unconscious. The belt around the neck is draped behind her so she hasn't tried to pull it tight herself. If she had, then I would've thought she'd be better off having the longer section at the front or tying it off somewhere so she could drop. There's nowhere for that. It's a room surrounded with sleek marble and no hooks or tie points. None required, as someone is on hand to fetch and carry. That said, if she was murdered, then the killer could have pulled it tight from the front and moved it around the back once she was in the water,' he said.

Nash mused on his words.

'They could have both been in the water when she was killed?' she offered.

'Possibly,' he replied, 'but why is she dressed if that was the case? Are you suggesting they entered the water clothed and then fought? There's no clothing in the changing room. Only a rogue slipper found under the lounger.'

'That's uncertain, and for Dr King to establish. On that note, I think it's time our pathologist was summoned, along with the rest of the forensic cavalry,' she said, standing up.

Moretti got up too. Both detectives were captivated by the image in front of them. Nash looked again at the body from where she stood. Sometimes it wasn't the ones covered in blood that resonated the most, it was the ones that appeared out of place that troubled her mind. Nash made the decision not to enter the water until Dr King was present. Chances were, he'd ask for the victim to be removed once photographed, to conduct an initial examination and confirm death. That wasn't within Nash's authority despite the fact the victim wasn't breathing. It wasn't lost on Nash that Petrov had made no effort to see if the victim was alive or call an ambulance. She would have to address that, along with finding the owner of the slipper. In her mind it felt pointless. It was probably Petrov's. After all, according to Middleton, he was the only one to discover the body and the footwear was reasonable to wear poolside.

Moretti left Nash and went to get his phone, which he'd left in the room Middleton had allocated to them. The meeting room was used by clients for business purposes and came equipped with state-of-the-art facilities, from drop-down screens to a secure server they could use to communicate with associates around the world, and Middleton had supplied them with a key card to secure it.

Nash returned to the meeting room and joined Moretti.

'It's all arranged,' he said.

Nash nodded, removing her white suit, and selecting a new one ready for when Dr King arrived.

'Strange place, isn't it?' Nash said.

Moretti nodded. 'One of the rare inside scenes where I don't have to duck under doorways or stoop for the entire examination,' he said.

Nash smiled and threw him a new white suit. She carried one for Moretti as his were an unusually large size due to his height and she never wanted to be at a scene and her DS be without forensic clothing. He had his own Tyvek suits in his bag, but she was feeling generous.

'While we're waiting, let's get on to the Diplomatic Protection Group. See if the DPG register shows Petrov having diplomatic immunity. Better bottom that line of enquiry out before I decide how to approach him,' she said.

Moretti nodded and Nash sat in a comfy two-seater Chesterfield chair while she waited for him to complete the call. Her mind was alive with what needed to be done within the golden hours she had before her. The key hours of any new investigation, where the clock was ticking down to retrieve any vital evidence. Drug and alcohol levels were diminishing in the blood, CCTV could be destroyed, witnesses could flee or clam up. A suspect could disappear or destroy vital evidence.

Despite the closed scene, she always kept an open mind with any investigation. Just because the gates were closed when they arrived didn't mean they were always secure. The fact Petrov was hiding behind immunity within a safe room didn't mean he'd killed her. He had a lot of explaining to do though.

CHAPTER FOUR

Dr King's attendance was brief but thorough. He explained to both Nash and Moretti that the victim was already dead when she'd entered the water. This information told Nash that there could be another scene and why the poolside was undisturbed. Dr King intimated that he would need more time to examine the body, away from Heath Hall. He'd conduct toxicology tests in addition to a physical examination. All he confirmed to Nash was that, from his initial examination, there were no obvious contusions to the victim's skull. The belt was looped through the buckle. Track abrasions were evident on her neck and told him that force had been applied through the constriction of the belt from the rear. Whether this was the cause of death was too early for him to confirm.

Nash felt King was vague with his feedback. This was unlike him. Dr King was a leading London pathologist, his career one of steadfast resolve from scene to court. The fact he was reluctant to suggest a possible cause of death bothered her. He wouldn't even provide an approximate time she might have died. He said he would only offer this once he'd obtained information on the average temperature of the room and water. Nash valued Dr King attending her scenes as once he'd left, she could formulate an investigative strategy beyond guesswork.

Middleton had performed her role with aplomb, providing Nash with a comprehensive printout detailing the water and room temperatures, as requested by Dr King. The pathologist had already left, but at least Nash had what was required to assist his autopsy. Middleton had insisted the temperatures were accurate. Robust monitoring systems were in place within Heath Hall, she'd said, particularly in the pool area. This was to ensure they were maintained consistent throughout the year. If a guest were to complain about the coolness or otherwise of the room or water, Middleton would take great pride in showing the data.

The post-mortem was confirmed by Dr King for 4 p.m. Earlier in the day was out of the question. Dr King's tables were full, following a multiple stabbing in a shopping centre the previous evening. Before he left, he handed Nash an embossed name badge in a clear evidence bag. Not any old backstreet badge printer's effort, but a plate of precious metal with the name "Charlotte Harrington" engraved upon it. There was nothing else on the body other than a pair of earrings and a silver bracelet which were nondescript in appearance but added a touch of elegance and sophistication to the victim's attire.

Petrov was still to be spoken to, as were his security team. A resident chef and Middleton were also on the list of initial investigative lines. Nash felt the list was shy of staff she'd come to expect would be employed in such a setting. She'd confronted Middleton with her thoughts on the subject and Middleton had been vehement that the staff on the list she'd presented were the "essential" indoor staff on duty since last night.

Nash sat in her newly designated incident room. The room Middleton had provided was good enough and a cut above what she was used to. With the delicate balance that staff and politically sensitive enquires required, she considered it a bonus. Many SIOs would have baulked at the notion of conducting an investigation from within the walls of the crime scene, but they weren't DI Pippa Nash. Nash saw the offer as an opportunity. A chance to keep the pressure on the household while the initial enquiries were conducted. If the information Middleton had provided were to be believed, then the killer may still be on the premises. Nash ran over the events in her mind: a Russian-sounding male had called the police saying that a body was found in a swimming pool, she appeared to be dead and their attendance was required.

When she and Moretti had arrived, the large main gates that spanned the driveway to Heath Hall were shut. A security guard, whom Nash now surmised to be one of Petrov's team, stood on the other side. By all accounts no one had entered or left the area prior to the response officer's arrival. The officer had contacted the uniform inspector to garner support and assist in gaining access to the property. Petrov was calling the shots here, of that Nash was in little doubt. The security were his personnel and acted on his instructions regardless of what police wished or the laws they sought to apply.

'Any joy from the Diplomatic Protection Group?' Nash said to Moretti, who was busy typing away on his secure laptop, a means of remote working employed within the Metropolitan Police's Homicide Command. It meant detectives could use their respective laptops to update the incident room's HOLMES system. It also meant they could work anywhere, but that's something Nash didn't embrace. She liked to interact with her team in person rather than by email or video call.

Moretti turned from his screen. 'Alex Petrov has immunity. I've been sent written confirmation beyond the verbal authority from the DPG's operations room. That's all we need,' he said, stretching his legs, arms behind his head.

Nash smoothed an eyebrow as she thought. 'It's not the end of the world. Let Petrov sweat a bit before we speak with him. We'll fit in some legwork with the other staff and see what their movements were. Let's get Ma'am Middleton in here and ask her a few questions about Charlotte Harrington. We'll need to inform next of kin... poor woman,' Nash said.

There was a light tap on the door. Nash got up and walked over to the only entrance and exit to the room.

'Ah, we were just coming to find you,' Nash said to Middleton who was stood in the open doorway, armed with an assortment of pastries on a silver tray balanced upon a matching hostess trolley.

'Luckily for you, the chef had prepared these. He asked if I'd convey them to you,' she said, striding past Nash pushing the trolley over to the table where Moretti sat.

He scooted his legs in before the trolley could collide with him, sitting upright like a schoolboy caught sleeping by the teacher. His eyes locked on the decoration of baked goods. Cakes of all different sizes sat upon a triple-tiered stand.

'I'll bring coffee and more cream, if that's all right with you, Inspector?' Middleton said, her hands held in front of her in a low prayer.

'As you wish. I'm sure my sergeant will make good use of what's on offer,' Nash said, glancing at Moretti.

Middleton nodded and left.

'Good job George Sagona's at the office; he'd have scarfed this lot in one breath,' Moretti said, his mouth open in readiness of a fresh cream and jam scone.

Middleton returned with the pot of coffee and cream as she'd promised. She poured for everyone before sitting in a single leather tub chair, legs crossed at the ankles, side on to Nash. Nash pushed her coffee cup away across a teak coffee table that acted as a demarcation line between them and sat forwards, her Mont Blanc fountain pen poised above a page in her decision log.

Middleton took a sip of coffee before replacing the cup, awaiting Nash's opening line. Nash readied herself for what she expected to be a laborious exchange of words.

CHAPTER FIVE

'I'd like to ask you a few questions, Ms Middleton, all standard in these circumstances,' Nash said.

Middleton nodded. Moretti stopped eating, wiping excess cream from his stubbled upper lip before opening his laptop at a blank screen in readiness to record the conversation. He'd decided to remain at the main meeting table and let Nash have the floor. Nash hadn't invited him over and he took this to mean she had her bases covered and would request his full attendance should she require it.

'How are you after discovering such a tragedy on the premises?' Nash said.

'As I explained, I wasn't the one who discovered the body, Inspector. Mr Petrov was the unfortunate soul in that regard. I was informed of the details by his lead security man once Mr Petrov was safe,' she said.

'When I asked if you knew who was in the pool, you mentioned you might from the description of the hair. Who gave you that detail?' Nash asked.

Middleton shuffled in her seat, straightening her skirt.

'I am the head of staff at Heath Hall, Inspector. Like you, it's my duty to ask questions. I asked the head of Mr Petrov's security, and he didn't know. All he was prepared to confirm was that a woman with red hair was floating in the pool. I asked what he meant by floating. He said she wasn't breathing, she was dead. I requested he call the police. I felt it was inadvisable for me to do so. He knew more having witnessed the situation, whereas I hadn't,' she said. Her voice was steady, but Nash detected a clipped tone.

Nash made a few notes before continuing. 'I see. Do you have a name for the security person you spoke to?'

'I'm afraid not. We don't need to know, only Mr Petrov does. As you can appreciate, my staff will have little to do with any guests' security staff beyond ensuring they are comfortable while they are here,' she said.

Nash resisted commenting further on this and decided to pursue the path she'd mapped out.

'I have a name badge from the victim given to me by our pathologist, Dr King. Does the name Charlotte Harrington mean anything to you?' Nash asked, pushing a digital image of the name badge across the table that Moretti had printed from the room's digital colour printer.

Middleton breathed in deeply, before releasing her breath. It was a slow and deliberate act. Nash considered it was a practiced method Middleton employed to control any rising panic, or possibly natural distress.

'Oh dear, I had hoped my thoughts wouldn't be confirmed as such, Inspector, but yes – yes, I know, knew, Charlotte. She wasn't a staff member, as such. She was a freelance executive. Mr Petrov always used her services when he was in London,' she said. Her eyes pooled with tears. She blinked.

Nash looked at Moretti who took the hint. He got up and brought an ornate gold tissue box from the meeting table that he passed across to Middleton. Moretti chose to remain with the two of them in a seat next to Nash. He'd anticipated his change of location by bringing his laptop with him.

'Thank you,' Middleton said, taking one and delicately dabbing her eyes.

'Was there another person you'd considered it may have been?' Nash asked.

Middleton reflected. 'Yes, a member of the green staff, gardens and horticulture, but then she wouldn't have been dressed in a suit,' she said.

'A suit?'

'Inspector, I'd prefer it if you didn't try and play mind games with me. The badge in the photo is handmade. It isn't a cloth embroidered patch severed from a pair of off-the-hangar denim overalls. You asked if I knew Charlotte Harrington. I've confirmed I did. She was a woman of impeccable taste. If she was wearing that badge, then she would have been dressed in a handmade suit from a tailor in Savile Row.'

Nash sat back, tapping her pen on the pad before setting it down. Maybe she'd come across in a hostile way she hadn't intended. It wasn't every day you ended up in a mansion interviewing staff about a body floating in a swimming pool. Normally, it was a stabbing in the street. A scene destroyed by rain in the arse end of London with no witnesses.

Nash leaned forwards, hands loose at her knees. 'I must do my job, and like you, I have my ways. Some people like them – others don't. I'm here to establish who killed Charlotte Harrington. A job that's not being made any easier by the fact the resident, Mr Petrov, the person who found Charlotte's body, is protected behind a wall of plaster, steel, and diplomatic immunity. If I'm coming across as determined, then please understand that every minute wasted means vital evidence could be lost. At present I have a name badge with no formal identification. I'm minded we are looking at one and the same person though. You have my condolences,' Nash said.

Middleton sat up, raising her chin. Her defiant posturing relaxed within an instant. 'I want the same as you, Inspector. I won't let the good name of Heath Hall, or Charlotte Harrington, be tainted by murder,' she said.

Nash gave a weak smile that conveyed a certain distaste of where Middleton's priorities were concerned. Property first then the person. Nash needed Middleton onside for now. She could be her killer, after all, and playing a very fine game. It was too early in her investigation to isolate the one person who knew the layout of the home and the occupants. Nash sat back placing her log in her lap at a blank page.

'I'll need all the personal details you hold for Charlotte: roster of work, hours billed, places frequented while with Petrov, or any other work-related activity. Can you provide these?' Nash asked.

Middleton nodded. 'Anything deemed reasonable will be provided,' she said.

'Deemed reasonable?' Nash said.

'By Mr Petrov, Inspector. After all there may be visits of a discreet nature he wouldn't want divulging,' she said.

Nash glanced at Moretti who raised his eyebrows in response.

'Ms Middleton–'

'Mrs,' Middleton interrupted.

'Mrs Middleton… please deem any request proportionate, necessary, and reasonable in accordance with the law. I cannot be clearer. Any obstruction of my investigation will be treated with the full weight of legislation available to me, immunity applies to Mr Petrov, but not to you or the management of Heath Hall or those employed on their behalf. Now, as much as I appreciate that Charlotte Harrington was a freelance executive employed by Mr Petrov, she does not have the same immunity. Any records, held by you, I want. If I don't get them, I will ask my DS to attend court and obtain a search warrant in relation to evidence concerned in murder. I will rip apart every inch of Heath Hall if I must. Do I make myself clear?'

Middleton blinked. Her actions were slow, no tears present. Her forehead failed to crease despite her years, thanks to the quarterly sessions of Botox she enjoyed.

'I will endeavour to provide all the assistance I can,' Middleton said.

'Good. Let's start with the CCTV for the duration of Mr Petrov's stay. I know you have it. I imagine the internal system is covert more than overt,' Nash said.

Middleton lightly rubbed her nose, as though she were experiencing a bout of congestion. Her eyes pinched.

'Is there a problem?' Nash said.

Middleton picked up a glass of water from the table. She sipped and swallowed before replacing the glass on the table. Her eyes met Nash.

'There's no CCTV, Inspector. I checked. I knew it would be an obvious requirement for any investigation. It no longer exists. I searched for images from last night and it's blank. I checked on earlier dates and, I regret to inform you, they're the same. Gone. I ran a system check too. The scan showed the system to be active and to all intents and purposes, fit and healthy,' Middleton said.

Nash got up and began pacing the room.

'You must be able to identify who accessed the system and when? I can only surmise the setup is above and beyond one found in a typical London hotel,' Nash said, tempering her response.

'I'm afraid it will show myself as the one wiping it,' Middleton said.

Nash's eyes flared at Middleton's reply.

'Go on,' Nash said, curious to hear Middleton's explanation.

'I was remiss in leaving my access card on my office desk. Regretfully, I must admit it's swipe-only access to view and administer. Heath Hall is a luxury residence, Inspector, not a bolthole for the criminally minded. I don't carry every card with me and certainly not where Mr Petrov is concerned. He's not a rock star or some other mindless celebrity. He has his own team of highly trained close protection staff. CCTV is of little use to him, and he insists it is only used in certain areas of Heath Hall. Areas he's unlikely to attend, such as the kitchens and staff rooms. He knows all his staff. He insists on conducting his own vetting of Heath Hall staff too. Most irregular, but he pays above and beyond for the privilege of this attention to detail. Personal safety, Inspector, is paramount to him. This street exists for the wealthiest in the world. The last murder was in the 1980s, and that was never investigated properly, might I add,' Middleton said, by way of vindicating herself from her apparent lapse in efficiency.

'Well, times have moved on since the 80s, Mrs Middleton. This problem isn't one I need or anticipated would be an issue. I'll have the hard drive for the system removed for forensic examination. There's every chance that any footage recorded can be recovered,' Nash said.

Moretti typed the request for the inside team to get the forensic engineers off their arses and out to their scene.

'Who holds keys for the pool area?' Nash said.

'We issue smart cards for all staff and those in residence. They are programmed to access all areas of the premises other than the safe room. Only my card accesses the safe room,' she said.

'I see, so it's swipe access everywhere?' Nash said.

Yes, pretty much, apart from the greenhouse,' Middleton said.

Nash ignored the quip. 'I'll need a printout of all the access cards used for the pool area as well as the rooms for last night and this morning. Up until 6 a.m. will suffice for now,' Nash said.

Middleton fingered a bracelet on her wrist.

'Don't tell me they've been destroyed too?' Nash said.

Middleton nodded.

'Inspector, I'm most embarrassed. I'm responsible for the systems that manage such matters. To my shame, I insisted on having one card to access them all. I didn't wish to be walking around like a croupier, or gaoler,' she said, perplexed.

'Shall we have some more coffee?' Nash said.

Middleton reacted as though Nash were a guest, deftly clearing down the table of the previous offerings before leaving the room.

Nash sat back dropping her forehead to the polished walnut table. Closing her eyes, she wished they'd open upon the Cairngorms and not the walls of stone that surrounded her.

She lifted her head, to find Moretti. 'I think I need a smoke,' she said.

Moretti laughed. 'Pip, you gave up years ago, whereas I am bloody desperate,' he said, patting his suit jacket and feeling the outline of his pipe and pouch.

Middleton returned with a fresh set of coffee cups on a tray as Moretti got up.

'My sergeant wishes to have a smoke. Is there anywhere he can go?' Nash asked.

'Oh yes, I'll take you to the smoking room,' Middleton said, leaving with Moretti in tow.

As he passed, he gave Nash a light squeeze of her shoulder. It was going to be a long day.

CHAPTER SIX

Middleton led with the assured confidence of a lady who knew her home and role within it. Not out of subservience of any kind, but a genuine appreciation of her position within the walls of Heath Hall. A position she prided herself on. It was a sought-after role that came with many perks and one that was rare to find. Moretti casually observed the way she dominated the environment. Middleton was a good six foot in height and Moretti wondered whether Nash felt intimidated by her. Nash was feisty for her diminutive five foot six, but even Moretti felt small in Middleton's presence. He put his feeling of mild inferiority down to the setting rather than the woman herself, preferring the modesty of his houseboat to the grand environment of Heath Hall.

Turning right at the first landing, they swept past an array of side doors to various bedrooms, until they approached what appeared to be a library carved into a nook on the landing. Moretti wondered if this was the smoking zone. There were a couple of leather tub chairs and a small coffee table in between them. The walls were surrounded with ceiling-height dark wooden bookcases. A black metal ladder on a runner was available to be electronically summoned if a book was too high to access. No doubt a servant would do this. He couldn't envisage a guest mounting the metal rungs of the ladder to retrieve a book.

They stepped into the zone. Middleton approached a bronze bust of a bearded gentleman that sat upon a shelf. The bust appeared to Moretti to be of someone of historical importance, though whose it could have been lay beyond Moretti's limited knowledge of significant subjects from days gone by. He'd never been one for history unless it was about policing.

'I'll be fine from here, thank you,' he said.

Middleton turned from where the bust sat surrounded by leather bound tomes.

'This is a no-smoking area, Sergeant. I'm certain the room designated for such pursuits will be more to your liking,' she said, eyeing Moretti up and down as she spoke.

Moretti squinted. Middleton pushed on the head of the bust. It dropped back. Middleton produced a credit-card-sized pass. She held it against a tiny square screen that had now been revealed in the neck. There was a clicking sound and Moretti looked on as the book-lined wall began to open inwards revealing what, to him, amounted to heaven.

Middleton smiled. 'I thought you'd be impressed,' she said, stepping into the smoking room.

Moretti followed, slowly shaking his head at what he was witnessing. A secret lair for nicotine-addled minds. Cabinets of the finest tobaccos and cigars lined the walls of this inner sanctum. All of which were contained within temperature-controlled ecosystems. He stalked the room taking in a section of handmade pipes made of wood and clay, objects of intricate carving that made his Savinelli briar appear like a prize from a grab machine at a fun fair rather than the fine Italian import it was.

'Well, you certainly know how to impress a man,' Moretti said, his eyes transfixed on the interior of the room.

'I'll take that as a compliment,' she said, pulling out a drawer from a cabinet and removing a shallow box of hand-rolled, gold-tipped cigarettes. 'Would you mind if I joined you? I could do with a break.'

Moretti diverted his attention away from the cigars. 'Not at all,' he said, removing his tobacco pouch and pipe as he sat.

'Please, allow me to offer you something from the Heath Hall cabinet, the finest tobaccos from around the world. All imported correctly, as per tax,' she said, a wry smile forming at her freshly painted lips.

Lips that Moretti hadn't appreciated until now. She must have applied some lipstick as she walked upstairs, he thought. Moretti wasn't usually a man to be conflicted by an offer of anything luxurious, especially when it was free and, by all accounts, paid for. He thought about what Nash would say before dismissing it. He had a job to do too and getting to know Middleton, he decided, was going to be a priority action he'd happily take on.

'I'll let you choose,' he said, happily letting Middleton demonstrate her skills as the perfect host.

Middleton opened the oak-framed external door to reveal a modern, glass-panelled, hermetically sealed unit. She made a display of selecting an appropriate tobacco before removing a leather-bound box and closing the door to the unit. She moved towards the pipe cabinet where Moretti was surprised to see her select the pipe he'd been enamoured with as he'd investigated the new surroundings.

'I thought you might enjoy the combination of the Churchill with this mild Scottish tobacco. It was one of his favourites,' she said, handing Moretti the pipe.

'Mr Petrov's a smoker?' he said, turning the pipe over in his hands, unsure of whether he wanted to use it. The pipe was clearly hand-carved, and Moretti didn't relish the invoice should he break it.

Middleton sat opposite him, crossing her legs, she ran her palms down her thighs, smoothing her skirt as she leaned into the armchair. The leather was as soft as a well-used tobacco pouch and Moretti felt it must have been commissioned to reflect the surroundings. To him it felt like he'd stepped into a gentlemen's club of old.

'Mr Petrov doesn't smoke,' Middleton said, interrupting Moretti's thoughts. 'I was referring to Winston Churchill, the original owner of the pipe you are holding,' she said, leaning for the silver lighter that sat upon a low table between them.

Moretti reacted with all the skill of an attentive host, thumbing the ornate shell until a flame danced from the wick. Middleton accepted his offer of a light, her cigarette neatly installed within an ivory holder. She leaned away, inhaling deeply before exhaling a fine wisp of smoke towards Moretti, an act Moretti found incredibly alluring.

He placed the Churchill down in its case and produced his own pipe. He'd use the tobacco though, and began the ritual of filling the bowl. As he did, he utilised the convivial atmosphere of the room to his advantage.

'So, how long have you worked here?' he said, tamping down the first layer of leaf.

'I lost my husband in 2015 – so ever since then,' she said.

Moretti didn't pass comment. 'I see, and you enjoy this line of work?'

Middleton thought for a moment. 'It's better than most jobs available to a woman of my age and skills, Detective. I'd had my fill of city firms who thought executive skill sets amounted to taking minutes and reminding the men when their wives' birthdays were,' she said.

Moretti noticed she was looking up and to the right as she spoke, a sign that the memories evoked were significant to the subject. Moretti had always considered most interview theory to be psychological bollocks but, looking at Middleton, he wondered whether she was yanking his chain or being truthful. He allowed her the moment of reflection before he continued.

'Did you work with Harrington – Charlotte, I mean?' he said.

Middleton's eyes returned to Moretti.

'Not as much as I would have liked. She was a bright girl, utterly professional in every aspect of her life, and a whizz with languages. That's why Mr Petrov insisted on having her with him. She knew London, as she was educated here. She has a flat in Chiswick. She could mix, unobtrusively, at various functions. She'd feedback anything she felt may be in the best interests of Mr Petrov. She was incredibly socially skilled. She confided in me once that Mr Petrov thought she'd make a good spy. She will be missed. I will miss her. She added brightness to what can be a dull home to inhabit, at times, despite the obvious grandeur,' she said.

Moretti waved the lighter over the pipe bowl until the red glow showed him the tobacco was lit. He took his time placing the lighter back on the table next to a matching dome-covered ashtray. Moretti felt more relaxed now and noticed a low hum. An extraction system had been triggered because of the smoke. Ingenious, he thought, before returning his attention to Middleton.

'Mrs Middleton, where were you last night?'

Middleton maintain her relaxed position in the chair. She inhaled on her cigarette and held the smoke before smiling and exhaling through her nose. The smoke drifted gently as she held her cigarette to the side, letting it waft beyond her. 'I was at home. Alone,' she added.

Moretti nodded. 'Where is home?' he said.

'Which one? I have a few properties, Detective.'

'Your main place of residence?' he said.

'Highgate Village, stone's throw from here,' she said.

'Is there anyone that can verify you were there?' he said.

'I was alone, Detective: on one's own, all alone, solitary, single, singly, solo, solus; on one's Jack Jones. I can't be clearer.'

Moretti pursed his lips. 'I have to ask,' he said. 'It would help if you could think of anyone that could verify where you were.'

Middleton re-lit her cigarette. 'Detective, I didn't murder Charlotte Harrington. I liked the girl. I wouldn't wish any harm upon her. I'm as keen as you to establish who killed her. I did see Mr Petrov, briefly when he returned to Heath Hall after dining at Claridge's. Once he'd dismissed me, I left and went home, by car, alone,' she said.

Moretti jabbed the air in her direction with the stem of his pipe, 'I hope that's the case, but you can see why I'd ask. You've acknowledged your card was used to access and delete the CCTV. If that wasn't enough, the times for door access have also been destroyed for last night and this morning. If it wasn't you using the card, who was it?' Moretti said.

'If we knew that, Detective, I wouldn't be subject to your line of questioning, would I?' An air of a chill to her voice displaced the warmth of the room.

Moretti pondered where else to go with the conversation. He noted Middleton's cigarette was running low and doubted she'd want another so soon after. This wasn't a prisoner in the holding cage enjoying a fag break prior to getting booked in custody. Middleton was going to be a challenge; of that, he had no doubt.

Moretti produced a business card and slid it across the table. 'If you think of anything, you can call me on this number – the mobile is on twenty-four hours, so don't hesitate to use it,' he said.

Middleton took it off the table and turned it over in her fingers before placing it on the arm of the chair. She didn't read it.

'I'd be grateful for that list of staff as soon as possible. DI Nash will wish to speak to Mr Petrov sooner rather than later,' Moretti said.

Middleton nodded.

'That won't be difficult. In addition to myself there was Charlotte, obviously, Derek, the chef, and Camilla would have been on duty until 2 a.m. Then you have Mr Petrov's security team: four in all. Two on duty, two off. Then there's the garden maintenance crew who work days, and the dog man, John McNeil, who works as and when requested. Other than that, I imagine it's not looking too great for Mr Petrov,' she said.

'Why would you say that?' Moretti said.

Middleton blew a gentle plume of smoke into the air, the grey accenting the rouge of her lips. 'He had a thing for Charlotte,' she said.

'What do you mean?' Moretti said, leaning forward.

'I mean, he wanted to get her into bed, Detective, but she was having none of it,' she said, shrugging.

Moretti sighed. 'It would have been good to have known this earlier,' he said.

'Well, you know now. I would appreciate your discretion as regards to whom this information originated from. I have a reputation to keep, and gossip isn't something I appreciate.'

'This is hardly gossip, it's a murder investigation, and I can't guarantee anything. How do you know this?'

Middleton rubbed her nose. 'Charlotte confided in me. She was finding it challenging to explain to Mr Petrov that there were boundaries in a close working partnership that she wasn't willing to go beyond.'

Moretti sat back in the chair and wagged the pipe stem in Middleton's direction. 'Go on,' he said.

Middleton paused and swallowed. 'I never saw Mr Petrov act inappropriately, Detective. I am astute when it comes to unwanted sexual advances. It's inescapable in my line of work. I don't stand for it and will always support my staff whenever I witness it, or it's brought to my attention, regardless of the client. I make no exception. This is why Charlotte confided in me.'

'When did she speak with you?'

Middleton breathed in deeply. 'Yesterday, before they left for Mr Petrov's embassy engagement and dinner at Claridge's.'

'How did you leave it with her?'

Middleton raised her eyebrows. 'That we'd speak again and formulate a plan to help her avoid any unwanted behaviour,' she said, stubbing out her cigarette before standing up.

Moretti sensed there was little point in pressing the issue further at this stage. He'd gained information she hadn't divulged when Nash had been speaking to her and saw this as a chance to return to the subject once he'd probed the other staff on their movements. He tapped out the dregs of the pipe's bowl into the ashtray and stood.

Middleton faced him. 'I prefer talking to men, Detective, especially men who smoke. Your inspector could do with learning from you how best to extract details from a person in an inquiry,' she said. 'Now, if you'll excuse me, I'll get you that list.'

They both left the informality of the smoking room for the formality of the main building, Middleton carrying the ashtray as the false door to the room opened then sealed behind them.

CHAPTER SEVEN

'What do I do with this?' Nash said as Middleton positioned a keyboard on the table in front of her, with what appeared to be a small toggle switch attached.

Middleton ignored Nash's question as she continued to fuss with the keyboard's position. She pressed a few buttons and a drop-down screen descended from a cavity in the far wall. Once she was satisfied with her efforts, she turned to address Nash.

'This will facilitate communication with Mr Petrov, Inspector. You can use the toggle switch to adjust the angle of the camera in the suite. Unless it's been fixed by the occupant, that is,' she said.

Nash waited until the screen crept down the wall. A solid-looking expanse of a panel that had a white dot blinking from its centre.

'So, if I can access Mr Petrov's camera feed, he can presumably access the camera and microphones within the room we're in too?' Nash said.

Middleton had turned her back to Nash while the screen clicked into place on the floor. She turned back once it was at floor level.

'No. The room we're in is designed for complete privacy. There is a switch to listen to the panic room, but it's one-way only. You can't expect people of power to conduct sensitive business arrangements as though they were at an open mic session. This isn't the Comedy Store, Inspector.'

Moretti stifled a laugh.

'Where are the microphones and cameras for this room?' Nash said.

Middleton gave a brief flicker of a smile before walking over to a locked cabinet. She punched in a keycode attached to a door that looked like a safe. She opened the thick panel and produced a protective case that wouldn't appear out of place on a battlefield. She strolled over to the meeting table then undid the lid and opened it before tilting the innards of the case towards Nash and Moretti, much like a jeweller trying to entice a potential sale. Within the foam lining of the case sat a device like a large remote control with the addition of an integral colour screen.

'You're welcome to use this. I'm sure you're a familiar with such a device? This is the WAM-108T multi-band wireless activity monitor. I can show you how to use it, but the instructions are straightforward. The results you'll obtain will demonstrate my word is good, Inspector,' Middleton said, sitting down at the table.

Nash looked at the device and across at Moretti who wasn't making a good show of trying not to laugh.

'My DS will undertake the sweep of the room,' she said, sending Moretti's look of mirth into oblivion.

He pulled the case towards him before extracting the device as though it were contaminated. Nash pushed an instruction book across to him that was secreted in the cavity of the case's lid.

'When will Mr Petrov be available?' she said.

Middleton looked at her watch. 'I haven't been in touch with him. I was waiting for you to tell me when you wanted the video facility enabled. Mr Petrov is very self-sufficient thanks to the way the suite is stocked. By that, I mean he has food and drink. One of his men prepares everything for him, unless he orders from the house kitchen. He has no need to contact me, unless it's a housekeeping matter,' she said.

Petrov could be seen in the suite. He was dressed in a tracksuit that fitted his frame like a model. He sat quietly in an armchair cradling a mug. He appeared like a man who was staying in a flat with friends and they were preparing for how they would spend the day. Not a man who was under threat of death from forces unknown. Nash looked away from the screen to see Moretti waving the scanner around the walls of the room while observing the screen's readout. Eventually he sat back down and turned it off.

'From what I can tell, there's nothing of concern being displayed on this machine, aside from what's obvious. I've done the picture frames, electric sockets and anywhere I can think could conceivably hide a bug, but I'm no expert,' he said.

Nash nodded. She had to trust Middleton to some degree.

'Mrs Middleton,' she said, 'please contact Mr Petrov and inform him I wish to introduce myself.'

Middleton picked up a phone and pressed a single digit. Nash looked at the screen. The silence of their room was now invaded by the low buzz of a phone. The screen showed a male in a dark suit retrieve a handset. There was a brief exchange of words before the handset was passed to Petrov.

'The police wish to speak with you, sir, via the internal link. The link is live. Please place the phone down, thank you,' Middleton said.

Nash was impressed with the way Middleton gave no choice to Petrov. Petrov handed the phone to his security before sitting back, staring ahead.

'I trust you can see and hear me?' Petrov said.

'I can, thank you. I am Detective Inspector Nash, and my colleague is Detective Sergeant Moretti. We are from the Homicide Command of the Metropolitan Police,' Nash said.

Petrov nodded. 'So it is murder then, yes? So, I was right to be taken to this place while you find who committed such a brutal act,' Petrov said.

Nash blinked. 'I find the use of this panic room somewhat extreme, Mr Petrov, but you are where you are, and we are where we are. I have some questions that it is imperative are answered so that I can progress the investigation. Are you willing to answer them?' she said.

Petrov took a swig of his drink, holding the mug out to be refilled by the suited male. He placed the mug on a low coffee table and gestured with his hand in a swatting motion. Behind him another suit-clad male could be seen to exit the living area along with his colleague. Petrov waited until the door was quietly closed before leaning forwards.

'Inspector, I have sought legal advice. I am not prepared to discuss matters until my lawyer arrives. He is on his way and expected imminently. Now, if your country make a request with Russia to revoke my immunity status, and Russia agree, then I will have no option but to speak with you, subject to legal advice and the laws of your country. Until then, I will exercise my right of diplomatic immunity, after all what's the point of having it if we don't use it, eh?' Petrov sat back, his arms draped across the chair.

Nash took a moment before replying, aware that she wasn't in a position of strength. But she would do things the way she always did, diligently and utilising everything she could muster. She'd establish who killed Charlotte Harrington, with or without the help of Petrov.

'Very well. As you don't wish to cooperate with my investigation, I'm left with managing with what I have. I'm to understand from Mrs Middleton that the suite is self-sufficient. That's a bonus as you won't feel the need to leave your chosen place of safety. As for your lawyer, it's obvious to me that you have access to lines of communication. The house is my crime scene. Your lawyer will not cross the cordon I have in place. Until I have anything further to communicate, do you have anything you wish to say?'

Petrov smiled. 'Do not underestimate me, Inspector, I make a dangerous enemy. I will act in accordance with the laws of your country. Laws designated to protect me, a visitor. You would be prudent to familiarise yourself with what they are. Until we speak again, or not, good day,' he said.

Nash nodded at Moretti, who pressed a button next to the one he'd seen Middleton operate, and the screen went blank.

'You're keeping Mr Petrov against his will in Heath Hall?' Middleton said, eyebrows raised and eyes wide.

'No. I'm ensuring his safety is maintained as per his wishes,' Nash said.

'Well… it's most irregular,' Middleton commented, darting a glance at Moretti.

'It's called crime scene management. Now, in relation to that, I have some calls to make and would ask that you leave this room. Don't leave the building. I'd like the men at the gates to be informed they are to be closed and only opened on my say-so,' Nash said.

'Will you require access to the CCTV room to monitor your request?' Middleton offered.

'That would be useful, thank you,' Nash said, turning to Moretti.

She waited until Middleton had exited the room, the sound of her heels echoing across the stone floor.

'What a cluster fuck this is turning out to be,' Nash said, much to Moretti's surprise.

'Foul language? Someone's rattled your cage, Pip,' he said, smiling.

Nash reflected on the conversation with Petrov. He was a self-assured man, of that there was little doubt. From his body language, Nash assessed he didn't know where the cameras in the room were situated – his eyes roved as he spoke, as though seeking a camera to talk to. He had every right to say what he did and react so. She was also aware that he could be communicating with anyone, and she'd struggle to intercept or monitor those calls. Not that she needed to at this stage, but she was aware that her crime scene was being taken over by status and power beyond her control and she didn't like it. Wealth talked in the UK, and especially foreign wealth. Charlotte Harrington deserved better by all accounts and Nash made a pact with herself to ensure she'd find her killer by all legal methods open to her.

CHAPTER EIGHT

Nash left Moretti to manage the scene at Heath Hall. She'd been summoned by Commander Allen, head of the Homicide Command, to attend New Scotland Yard to brief him on the status at the property. Nash hadn't wished to leave her scene. The lawyer for Petrov hadn't arrived, and Nash suspected he'd been contacted by Petrov and advised of their conversation. Charlotte Harrington's body had been removed. Nash had waited until the victim been taken from the premises before she left. She had weaved her way through the press gathering at the gates of Heath Hall just as a firm were arriving to drain the pool. Moretti had been busy making arrangements to facilitate her briefing to the commander.

She was collected by one of her DCs who dropped her at New Scotland Yard. She'd used the journey to get updates on her inside team's work and the actions Moretti had been requesting while they were at Heath Hall. The list of staff had been drafted by Middleton and passed to the intelligence desk where each person listed was being researched. A contingent of detectives had been dispatched to conduct house-to-house in The Bishops Avenue, many volunteering just to see who lived in the mansions close to the venue. Nash wondered how disappointed they'd be to discover they were occupied by builders or security staff who spent most of their time concentrating on their phones.

The Thames was choppy as she stared across at the river from the front of the Met's corporate building. The police launch drifted close to Westminster Bridge. There'd been a spate of people jumping from the bridge, according to the national news. She made use of the fresh air to clear her head of the oppressive atmosphere of Heath Hall. Time to compose herself before her meeting with Commander Allen. It was rare to be called to his office. Nash knew the shit had hit the fan when she'd taken the call from his personal assistant who'd been adamant the commander wouldn't be coming to her, and she should come to him, live crime scene or not. In other circumstances she'd have argued it out, but on this occasion she appreciated the sensitivities surrounding Petrov were above and beyond the norm. The diplomatic fallout would no doubt have been initiated once Petrov's status had been checked. Once the reasons for the request were given, Petrov's embassy would have been informed too.

She entered New Scotland Yard and once she'd run through the standard security protocols, she took the stairs to the commander's office. Many others of his rank were based at Putney and there were rumours he was only there as he was next in line for Commissioner once the current face retired. Nash breezed to the floor the commander's office was on and went directly to his reception area where she waited. After five minutes, the door opened. A contingent of suited and flustered individuals emerged. Most looked drained and Nash surmised they'd all been tasked with various jobs they could've done without. The commander held the door for the last to leave and nodded at Nash to join him.

Clive Allen was a career climber. He'd made his sergeant's exam coincide with the completion of his constable's probation, a good use of the accelerated promotion scheme. He took no prisoners. Literally. It was a trait evident to anyone who'd been unfortunate enough to work with him at street level. He moved with confidence behind a leather-topped writing desk, in stark contrast to how he reacted in a fight. A carved wooden chair with matching leather back and seat finished off the stately feel of his office furnishings. He plonked himself down in the chair before reaching for a fountain pen that sat in an ostentatious-looking pen holder. Stripping a sheet of cream paper from a jotter, he made a flustered note before placing the pen on a leather ledger, cap off. Nash sat opposite him in a cloth-covered chair that despite her diminutive frame made her sink slightly. Nash guessed the furniture was all designed to increase Allen's need for power. He must always be seen to be above those that entered his lair, even when seated. He wasted no time in getting to the point of Nash's summons.

'What in the hell's going on at Heath Hall, Inspector? That contingent of senior management you witnessed leaving have all had their days tipped upside down thanks to Mr Petrov's apparent incarceration. I've been barraged with requests from the commander of the Diplomatic Protection Group since the early hours and a diary that's been wiped clean to accommodate a meeting with the Foreign Office at noon. I'm not impressed, Inspector. I understand Mr Petrov, according to his lawyer, is being detained against his will and that you have the entire house and staff on lockdown,' Allen said.

Nash waited to ensure Allen had finished. 'Is there any tea or coffee left? It's been a trying morning,' she said, nodding at a hostess trolley topped with two silver urns that had seen better days, and a host of white porcelain mugs embossed with the MPS crest.

Allen sat back, before wiping his widow's peak with the palm of his hand.

'Inspector, are you being flippant?'

'No, sir. I'm being honest, I'm parched,' she said.

Allen pushed a button on his desk phone.

'Paul, come in please and facilitate the drinks, thank you.' He depressed the button and sat back.

The main door opened, and Allen's uniform PA strode over to the trolley, poured out two coffees, added milk, and placed them in front of each officer before leaving. Nash was pleased to see she'd diffused what she'd assessed could have turned into an incendiary discussion that needn't be. She hated Allen, as did most of the homicide command, but she appreciated that with every rank came increased accountability. She'd expect Moretti to support her and despite her apathy towards Allen, she wished him no harm.

'Sir, I have to say that coming here, and leaving my scene, isn't conducive to progress with the current situation at Heath Hall. I am managing a murder within a home on the wealthiest street in London with a man who found the victim's body and subsequently locked himself in a panic room claiming diplomatic immunity. As it stands, the CCTV system has been wiped by persons unknown, and I won't know the cause of death until later today. What I do know is that Charlotte Harrington was killed before she went in the water. Where, is a mystery. So, yes – until I can establish a succinct perimeter for my scene, I'm taking a view that the house and grounds are within my domain unless evidence suggests otherwise. I'm sure you understand having investigated many murders yourself,' Nash said, knowing full well Allen hadn't sniffed an incident room as an investigator in his service, let alone been to a scene of violent death.

Allen rotated his chair towards a vast window with a view across the Thames, rocking the seat on his heels, fingers steepled in front of his nose. 'Pippa, can I call you by your first name?'

Nash nodded.

'You may not be aware just how sensitive this inquiry has become. Mr Petrov is a significant figure back in

Russia, a supporter of the United Kingdom, if you will.' He paused and turned to face Nash.

'He waves a Union Jack on the King's birthday?' Nash said.

Allen rose to his feet. 'Enough. You need to remember where you are, Inspector. There are issues of national security at stake, hence that meeting before ours. Alarms have been sounded abroad and Russia are asking why a citizen of theirs is being detained at his place of residence. Do I need to spell this out? There's nothing to say he killed the girl and finding the body doesn't make him a suspect.'

Allen sat back and retrieved the pen and paper. Nash remained impassive. This wasn't a meeting to be briefed, it was a moment for Allen to deliver a message – leave Petrov alone and vacate Heath Hall.

'Sir, with all due respect, I cannot close a crime scene until I'm satisfied all forensic lines of inquiry have been exhausted. I'm way off that,' Nash said.

Allen looked up. 'I've spoken with your DCI and he's fully on board with my suggestion, I'll leave it for you to speak with him, but I felt it best you hear it direct from me too,' Allen said, tapping the pen on the pad of paper.

'There was a small part of me hoping this meeting was to discuss additional resources… and yet I'm not surprised to be given this alternative message. What would you do, sir? If this were your crime scene?' Nash said.

Allen remained focussed on the world outside his office. Nash wondered if he'd not heard her or was choosing to simply ignore the question. It wasn't long before he responded, 'What I would do, in your position, is neither here nor there. You have been informed of my views and I expect them to be adhered to. You won't be a homicide inspector forever, Pippa. Think about your future.'

Nash placed her empty cup down on the desk and stood up. Allen was about to stand, but Nash was already at his door.

'My DCI will update you on my actions from here, sir. As for my future, I decide that. Good day,' she said, exiting his office and leaving his door open. As she passed his PA's desk, he glanced up at her and Nash noticed the live call button on his landline was on.

'I wish I had the balls to address him like that,' he said as Allen's voice summoned him again.

'You have a voice. Use it,' Nash said as she left.

CHAPTER NINE

Moretti attentively observed Yvonne Campbell, the SOCO, as she examined the water filter that had been extracted from the drained pool. An arc light illuminated Yvonne's area of operation at the pool's edge. Although the natural light was reasonable for a crime scene examination, she'd insisted Moretti get an independent source erected while she made a closer inspection of the pool's filters. She didn't intend to examine them in situ, but she could assess whether there was anything suitable within them first, before securing them for transport to the lab. With forensic resources stretched to capacity, every exhibit submitted had to be deemed necessary and worthy of scientific scrutiny. A job Moretti was glad someone else was doing.

He left her to it and went outside for a smoke. Not at the front of the building – that was currently occupied by the media and their various long lenses, fully extended, in a bid to capture an exclusive shot. He knew from experience how well these cameras could pick out detail. Details of exhibits being brought out of a scene, for one. The most expensive microphones could also detect conversations from a distance. This was why he always insisted that blue-covered crates were used for all clear exhibit bags leaving a scene and that his detectives kept their mouths shut in the vicinity of the press. There was nothing the press wouldn't record or use to gain advantage in their weary world of creating drama.

Middleton had arranged for him to use McNeil's cabin, a Scandinavian wooden unit with an outdoor kennel and run attached. The dog man's cabin wasn't an Ikea job, either. This one was kitted out so that McNeil could stay over if the guests were many and the need dictated he remain on site. Moretti took his time as he strode along a shingle path that weaved neatly alongside a clipped beech hedge. The hedging was designed to ensure the greenhouse and garden staff were separated from the main lawn. You couldn't have guests seeing the essential staff at work, not while they sought to relax.

Moretti wasn't a garden guy. He had a small space on his boat that Tabatha, a neighbour and close acquaintance of his, had used as an herb garden. That was until Moretti realised the plants she was cultivating under a small cloche and heat source weren't compatible with his line of work. Moretti preferred to experience the great outdoors away from London. The Lake District was a favourite haunt of his. He thought about taking a break once this investigation was complete. His musings were distracted by the formation of a police search team that fanned out across the lawn area beyond the hedge.

Nash had requested he organise this, as she was keen to establish where her first scene may be. Dr King had stated that the victim was dead prior to entering the pool. Moretti had remonstrated with Nash about the futility of the search operation – he'd have to brief the search leader as to what they sought, and could think of nothing, since the ligature supposedly used to kill Harrington had already been recovered. He knew Dr King hadn't provided written confirmation of this, but he hadn't intimated they should seek any other murder weapon at this stage. Moretti considered it was Nash's way of keeping the scene wide while Petrov stewed in his panic room of plenty.

Moretti breached a corner of the hedge where the leading lines of the expertly pruned foliage opened upon a large greenhouse and allotment area. He could see the log cabin Middleton had referred to. To Moretti's astonishment, there was a male sat on a swing seat under a slate roofed porch. The male was dressed all in black; cargo trousers paired with matching bomber jacket and military style lace-up boots. The jacket was festooned with various pockets. At the man's boots lay a spaniel, whose own glossy coat blended in fittingly with the male. On sensing Moretti's approach, the dog's head popped up from his outstretched paws. Moretti slowed his pace to observe the pair. He hadn't requested a police search dog unit to assist in the investigation. He wondered if the POLSA search team leader had done so as the grounds were vast, and a dog could give an indication of a suspect's scent across the lawns to the pool.

The clothing the male was wearing wasn't police issue. As he got closer Moretti could make out a Velcro patch with "K9 Security" stitched in yellow on a dark background. Below this was another patch with a thin blue line that ran vertically across the rectangle. The male had been focussed on his boot's stitching. As he noted the change in his dog's attention, he too turned in the direction of Moretti.

Moretti approached the deck. 'Who are you?'

'I could ask the same thing, mate,' the man said.

Moretti moved the side of his suit jacket to display his warrant card, which was folded between his crisp white linen shirt and the top of his grey flannel suit trousers. The male nodded and closed his eyes, before opening them again and standing.

'John McNeil, K9 Security for Heath Hall. I'd been waiting for someone official and here you are,' he said, holding out his hand to be shaken.

The spaniel began whimpering with excitement as Moretti stepped up onto the decking and shook McNeil's hand.

'How long have you been here?' Moretti said, with a tentative lilt to his voice.

'I was working last night so I slept here,' he said, nodding back at the cabin.

'You've been here all night?' Moretti said.

'Yes, I was asked by the management to remain in residence for this client. The client, Mr Petrov, had been very specific about his needs. Gold service. All good money. Way better than when I was with your lot,' he said, ruffling his dog's head.

'So, you've been here since when?' Moretti said, ignoring McNeil's remark about being ex-police, but storing it in his mind for the inside team to research.

'I arrived yesterday morning. Swept the grounds with the dog before heading here. I was due a final sweep last night, around 6 p.m., but Middleton said Mr Petrov was away on business and dismissed me. You lot arrived this morning, so I thought I'd better stay put and wait for you to see me. I'm surprised Mrs Middleton didn't mention I was here,' McNeil said.

Moretti shook his head. It wasn't what he wished to hear. A person within the grounds neither he nor Nash had been made aware of.

'How did you get here?' Moretti asked.

'By van. It's one I use for work, parked below ground in the garages,' he said.

Moretti took out his pipe and pointed with the stem at a spare chair. McNeil nodded and they both sat down. Moretti tried to get his mind to focus on what he was learning. A member of outside staff had been free to drift about the gardens and could have gone anywhere had he not stumbled across him. If Nash were to find out, she'd hit the roof. The inside staff were situated in their break room awaiting her return. Once she was back, they'd get to work on establishing their movements.

'Are there any others out here I should be aware of?' Moretti said, lighting his pipe before inhaling a mouthful of smoke and expelling it skywards. The grounds looked magnificent from where they were sitting, but Moretti couldn't help wondering how easily someone could gain access despite the obvious security.

McNeil leaned forwards, and the leather tracking lead that encircled his shoulder and body moved stiffly away from his chest.

'I'm it, I think. The green staff are gone. Due back this morning, but obviously that isn't going to happen. Is it Petrov?' McNeil said, looking across at Moretti.

'What do you mean, is it Petrov?'

'Is he injured, or worse?' McNeil asked, concentrating on the search team who'd come into view.

Moretti paused, choosing to take in McNeil's relaxed disposition. Unusual, he thought, for a man whose job was to secure the grounds only to discover he'd failed in his duty.

'No, it's not Mr Petrov. He's in the panic room,' Moretti said, waiting to see McNeil's reaction.

McNeil nodded, his shoulders dipping at the revelation. Moretti hoped Nash would get back quickly, as he needed her here. It wasn't that he lacked confidence in his scene management, just that the environment wasn't part of his life experience. He couldn't take in how one man could demand so much of others. So what if Petrov was loaded, why was he so concerned about his own safety to go to what Moretti saw as extremes in terms of personal security? Especially when it hadn't worked.

He let the silence between himself and McNeil linger while he reflected on where they were at in the inquiry. Harrington had been seen by Dr King and removed from the pool. The pool was drained of water and Yvonne was diligently undertaking her own examination of the filter system. CCTV was apparently useless, but the technical staff had attended and removed the hard drive for the system. Moretti had expressed his disappointment that they couldn't perform the operation on site, but he'd been told that wasn't possible without any reasonable explanation other than they had a remit for where they worked and the operator was sticking to his "remove to peruse" prerogative. The post-mortem was still going ahead at four o'clock. Everything was in hand as far as could be. He appreciated why Nash was keeping things tight. It was a delicate situation. Nash getting summoned to Commander Allen's office could only mean grief.

McNeil coughed and stood up, stretching his arms above his head. 'Alright if I run the dog?' he said.

Moretti looked at where the search team were currently working and back at the spaniel.

'I've a few more questions before you do that,' Moretti said.

McNeil nodded and sat back in the swing seat, where he leaned in the direction of Moretti, hands folded loose at his knees.

'I've nothing to hide, ask away.'

'When was the last time you saw Mr Petrov?'

'I thought he was alive?'

Moretti waited.

'He spoke to me when he arrived. He was with a bodyguard. It was unusual to have him address me directly. Normally he leaves any instructions for me with Mrs Middleton. He was asking about what type of dog I was using, and his bodyguard was keen to fuss her too. I told him she could search for drugs, guns, and bombs. He was happy with that and asked that I be proactive in my searching. I took that to mean be thorough and cover as wide an area as I could.'

'Did that mean inside and out?' Moretti said.

'I only do the private areas once prior to arrival. Communal as and when I assess it fit. Outside I run the dog regularly, in case of intruders, mainly. With the celebrity clients there are always groupies trying to get close as well as the press,' he said.

'But with Petrov that wouldn't be the case,' Moretti said.

'No, you're right, but Mr Petrov is classed, by Mrs Middleton, as a high-value client, so whatever he asks for he gets, in terms of security arrangements and providing they're legal. There's no smoking gun here, Detective, not that I've found anyway,' he said.

'Can your dog track?' Moretti asked.

'She's not the best tracker I have, but yes, she can do a good enough job for the purposes needed here. At least I thought she could until now.'

'How so?' Moretti said.

McNeil looked to the floor. His dog lifted her head, and he ruffled its skull. 'Well, whoever committed the crime must have got in and got away and I haven't found out how yet. Call it professional pride, Detective.'

Moretti raised his eyebrows. 'Okay, that was a useful chat, cheers. Stick to the allotment area. The police team have searched there. I'd prefer if you remain at the cabin until my DI gets back then we'll speak again.'

'Sure,' McNeil said, patting his thigh for the spaniel to join him.

As McNeil stepped off the deck, Moretti's phone vibrated with a text from Nash. She was in their makeshift incident room. Moretti tapped out the dregs of tobacco from the bowl of his pipe and made his way back to the main house, hoping she was here with news that would assist the investigation. In the back of his mind, he doubted she was.

CHAPTER TEN

Nash sifted through a decision log Moretti had been compiling. The research on Charlotte Harrington revealed nothing of concern. The house-to-house was a negative result in terms of any potential witnesses. She was happy with the actions he'd managed while she'd been seeing Commander Allen at New Scotland Yard.

Moretti arrived, pacing across the floor as he purposefully entered the room.

'You look troubled,' Nash said as he slumped into his chosen seat and powered up his laptop.

'Look, there's been a development but not one you're going to be happy with,' he said.

Nash raised her eyebrows.

'I was taking a smoke break when I bumped into the Heath Hall dog man, John McNeil. He's been here the entire time we have! He's camped in a cabin he uses at the rear of the gardens. He says he was on site yesterday, and I believe he would have been about when Harrington was alive. He indicated he'd stayed the night and that Middleton would have been aware of this,' Moretti said.

'Did you speak to him about what's happened?' Nash said.

Moretti palmed his mouth. 'I kept conversation light and loose. He did allude to Petrov and a bodyguard talking to him at the cabin. Petrov took an interest in what McNeil's spaniel could search for and asked him to be vigilant. I didn't say who'd been killed or how. Just didn't feel right with him. He's not being evasive as such, but I don't think he's being entirely honest either. A hunch more than fact. He'll stay at the cabin until we need him.

There's a police search team there. He alluded to being ex job too,' Moretti said.

Nash took hold of the phone on the desk, picked it up and pressed zero. 'Mrs Middleton, a word if you will, in our room,' she said, not waiting for a response.

Middleton promptly entered having been ensconced in her office next door. 'Would you like some refreshments?' she said, striding further into the space.

'I'd like to know who else might be wandering around the grounds that we don't know about? Staff who were here yesterday and stayed overnight,' Nash demanded.

Middleton didn't bat an eyelid at Nash's vitriolic questioning.

'By that, I take it you've met Mr McNeil from K9 Security?' Middleton's tone of voice was even and matter of fact.

'My sergeant had the pleasure of discovering his presence, yes. Why weren't we informed he'd stayed overnight and had been here when Harrington was on the premises?' Nash said, her manner calmer. She had Middleton on the ropes, or so she thought.

'I understand your dismay at this apparent oversight. However, I only knew of McNeil's stay when I went to the basement car park and recognised his van. I wouldn't always take note of his comings and goings, but he was parked in the wrong bay, so my attention was drawn to this,' she said.

Nash composed herself before replying, 'Why were you in the car park?'

'I was ensuring Mr Petrov's security team had space for their vehicles.'

'Are there any other people I should know about who were present yesterday and aren't in the staff break room with the others?' Nash enquired despondently.

'None. The list I provided is complete and I apologise for the omission of Mr McNeil. It's been a challenging time for us all, Inspector. Will there be anything else?'

Nash nodded. 'Have the chef, Derek White, brought through please,' Nash said.

Middleton returned Nash's nod of dismissal and left the room.

'It's time for answers and not from the lady of the manor. No more surprises, Nick. This inquiry needs to be expedited quickly,' she said.

Moretti looked perplexed. Nash was a stickler for thoroughness. Never one to be rushed, or to pressure her staff when an investigation required a deliberate and effective response.

'You don't want to start with John McNeil?' Moretti said.

'Not yet. You've spoken to him and that's good enough for me. Make sure he's on the staff research list though,' she said.

Moretti turned to his keyboard where he tapped out a message to George Sagona, their office manager, before hitting send. A swooshing noise leaked from his computer.

'Done. How was the meeting?' Moretti said, keen to hear the latest from the ivory tower.

Nash sighed. 'As you have no doubt surmised, it was all about Allen covering his arse to protect the prospect of his future promotion to Commissioner of the Metropolitan Police. Petrov appears to be a man whose influence has a global reach. Especially where the economic climate of the UK is concerned. So much so, Commander Allen wants Heath Hall turned over to Middleton so that Petrov can move about with impunity. Over my dead body,' Nash said.

'I could do without you getting added into the mix, one death here is enough,' Moretti replied.

A light tap on the meeting room door stopped their conversation. Before Nash could respond, a diminutive male dressed in crisp chef's whites entered the room. Derek White struck Nash as rather timid for a chef. Not that every chef was aggressive or hostile, but the kitchen environment was a tough gig for anyone, and Nash wondered how someone who appeared, on first impressions, to have so little charisma could cope with the clientele who'd rent this space and no doubt be extremely demanding.

'Please, take a seat,' Nash said, offering White the only spare chair opposite Nash and Moretti.

Nash produced a single sheet of A4 paper and ignoring White scanned down the brief list.

'Derek White? Is that you?' she said, placing the staff list Middleton had provided face down on the table.

White shuffled in his seat. 'Yes, that's me… I have to say, I'm in a state of shock so do bear with me.'

Nash could see his skin pallor matched the stark paleness of his clothing. He rubbed his hands together as though kneading fresh dough.

'There's nothing to fear from us, Mr White, please relax. I do have a few questions to put to you, all routine in an incident such as this,' Nash said.

White dipped his head a couple of times. Perspiration on his high forehead caught in the overhead LED lights that clustered the ceiling.

'I would like to say, officer, that I was most distressed to hear that it was Ms Harrington who was discovered in the pool, most distressed. She is, was, a lovely human being – at least to me,' he said.

Nash used the air space to see if White would expand on his comment, but it soon became evident from the way he stared at the floor that he wasn't going to continue.

'You knew her well?' Nash said.

'Well enough to know she was different. She'd always make any requests for food in a civil manner, rather than acting as though a dog were preparing it for his master,' he said.

Nash made a note on a pad perched on her knee.

'Are you saying you're treated harshly here?' she said.

White took a deep breath. 'A chef is considered indispensable, but on occasions that can amount to being treated like a robot. By that, I mean capable of operating beyond my shift without a recharge. Ms Harrington understood this wasn't the case. That there was a human being at the end of the phone. I think she was the only one who did, and now she's gone, I work here when Mr Petrov is in town and occasionally when other clients can't bring their own chef with them. I'm not so sure I'll be back now. Not after this,' he said, looking down at the floor again.

Nash sat back, giving White some space. His behaviour had knocked her off guard. She'd decided to begin with the chef imagining he'd be a tough nut to keep focussed. Despite the current lockdown she'd imposed, someone was obviously busy prepping meals and snacks for those left behind. They'd had freshly baked cakes, after all. Nash noted that while she'd been with Allen, Moretti had acquired a cooked breakfast. A dinner plate sat on a hostess trolley smeared in dregs of yoke.

'What were your movements up until 6 a.m. today?' Nash asked.

White looked up. He sat back and clasped his hands together at his knees. This question he was evidently comfortable to answer.

'I arrived by taxi, last night. The client was out, so there was only the prep for the following day to consider. I did this and decided to read. At midnight Mr Petrov ordered food: a steak, rare, with salad, no dressing. I prepped this and it was delivered by front of house. That was it for the evening. I was due to prepare breakfast – but it never happened. Mrs Middleton informed me Mr Petrov was in the secure suite. She explained there'd been an incident that required police attendance and that Ms Harrington wouldn't be having breakfast either. I asked why, and she told me she'd been found dead in the pool.' White's voice faltered.

Moretti passed the box of tissues over and White availed himself of a single sheet.

'So, you were in the kitchen from the time you arrived until Mrs Middleton saw you this morning?' Nash asked.

'Yes, from 10 p.m. last night, until around 6 a.m. this morning,' he said.

'Who served the food last night?' Nash asked.

White looked up then back at Nash. 'Camilla. She was brought in for this client's stay as a regular staff member was sick. She took the food. I heard nothing more. I don't even know if it was enjoyed,' he said.

'Did Camilla return to the kitchen afterwards?' Nash said.

'No. She may have been dismissed by Mr Petrov. You'd have to ask her,' White said.

Nash tapped the pad with her pen. 'So you don't manage your kitchen staff, the client does?' Nash said.

'We'd cleared down. There was nothing left to be done,' he said.

'How do you access the house?' Nash said.

White blinked. 'I don't need access to anywhere other than the kitchen and stores. I accept certain deliveries if it involves fresh produce, but other than that there are staff who deal directly with the clients. I cook, that's my job, the kitchen is my domain,' he said.

'How do you get in the building?'

'I walk in.'

'There's no need to be facetious, Mr White. Do you get let in or can you access the house by other means?' Nash said.

White leaned forwards. 'I don't have an access card. I get let in the main gate where I walk around to the tradesmen's entrance that's invariably unlocked. That is until Mr Petrov arrives, then it becomes an intolerable burden to get to my kitchen. One of his bodyguards is posted to the door or is at least there in the knowledge I'm due to arrive. Once I'm in, the door's locked.'

'You seem quite distressed for someone who didn't really know the victim?' Nash said.

White sat back, head snapping forwards. 'Inspector, a human being has been killed at my place of work. Death may be an occupational hazard for the likes of you, but for me it's a rare occurrence. Ms Harrington was employed when Mr Petrov was in residence. That could be as long as a month, or as little as a weekend. You form a loose bond with certain individuals and Ms Harrington was one such person. Now, if that's all, I have work to do.'

With that White began to stand. Nash didn't stop him. She'd asked enough at this stage. Moretti showed White the door.

Nash waited for Moretti to sit back down before she spoke.

'Well?' Nash said.

Moretti rocked in his chair; legs flayed at the heels of a new pair of brown brogues.

'I guess we speak with this Camilla. At least she can confirm part of his account. Imagine working all day in a kitchen that, from what I can tell, has no natural light. You'd have to get outside at some point, surely? It's as though the core areas that run the house function below ground. Like working in a custody suite,' he said.

Nash got up and walked over to a hostess trolley and showed Moretti the silver coffee pot. He nodded and she poured.

'Not quite the microwave meals created there,' she said, 'but I see your point. It also means there's little opportunity for us to explore anyone seeing someone passing a window or any chance view that may appear out of the norm. This place has a certain regimented feel to it. White's a strange cookie. Doesn't do eye contact, and he's furtive. I appreciate being a chef is an active and intense role, but I wouldn't be surprised if he was on something to help him through the day. Not necessarily a prescribed something either.'

She handed Moretti a china cup before joining him at the oval meeting table. A leather-topped captain's chair enveloped Nash and reminded her of Allen's office setup. All pomp and no circumstance.

'Do you want the kitchen searched?' Moretti said.

Nash sipped her coffee. 'Let's wait until we know more,' she said.

'Why don't we pop the camera on and see what Petrov's up to?' Moretti said.

Nash mirrored Moretti's nonchalant sway, rocking the chair upon her black Orla Kiely mules, which she wished she hadn't bought as they weren't providing the comfort she required. She longed to be in a pair of trainers pounding the streets on a run. Not in the stuffy environs of Heath Hall desperately attempting to salvage something of her investigation.

'No. I'm not happy eavesdropping, Nick. Petrov's a shrewd cookie; who knows what technology he may have employed independently to Heath Hall's. Not worth the risk. We need to revert to good old-fashioned legwork to solve this one, even if the legwork is treading marble rather than tarmac and walkways on estates,' she said. 'Let's get this Camilla in and grill her.'

'Medium rare?' Moretti jibed.

'Christ – stick to the day job,' Nash said, smiling.

CHAPTER ELEVEN

Moretti scrolled through some brief notes on the screen of his laptop. Nash had given him the lead on this interview, always one to share the burden of leadership with her DS, her mantra being there's no *I* in team. The inside desk, at the incident room in Hendon, had been diligent undertaking the actions Moretti had dished out. One of them being to research the staff list, Camilla Rodriguez among them.

White's research package hadn't thrown up anything untoward. He'd not been arrested or come to notice of the police. Not that Moretti had expected to read anything different. As he scanned down his screen, he noticed Camilla Rodriguez was appearing to be cut from the same cloth. Pristine and unblemished in terms of any police history.

There was a record of police being called to her flat in Chiswick, but it was marked up on the report as "no offences disclosed, parties advised to keep the noise down". Moretti wondered what noise was being made as there was no report of a party. Her flat was a new-build, and he surmised the walls were thin. He rolled his index finger over the mouse wheel until the template ended. He shut the laptop lid and rubbed his cheeks. He needed a shave. Nash sat opposite making notes and occasionally using her pen to tap on the pad as she thought, a trait of hers Moretti found irritating especially when he was lacking in sleep. They'd had a busy run up to this new inquiry and he was feeling a holiday was due. Murder was keeping him from any leisure time.

'Are you ready to see Rodriguez?' he asked.

Nash stopped tapping and pushed her pad away. 'Yes, let's get her in.'

Moretti placed the call through to Middleton who was all too happy to be involved in the fetching and ferrying of staff.

Where White was a breeze, Rodriguez was a whirlwind. She strode into the room like she owned it and pulled a chair into place between Nash and Moretti, catching them off guard as they were now unable to use the table as a natural barrier. Moretti closed his eyes and let his stomach settle before he opened them again and attempted to regain the lost element of control Rodriquez had, intentionally or not, robbed them of.

'I'm DS Nick Moretti of the Homicide Command and this is DI Nash. I'll be asking you a few questions about your movements last night. You're not under arrest and free to leave if you wish,' he said.

Rodriguez smirked.

'Leave? Fat chance the way this place is run,' she said, biting on the edge of her thumbnail before dropping her hand in her lap as she stared at Moretti.

'What's your role here?' Moretti said.

Rodriguez shrugged. 'I thought you'd know that, Sergeant. Police 101 after interviewing the chef and I work with him? I don't normally work here, but Chef White brought me in for the job. We've worked together before,' she said.

Moretti made a note of this. 'We've spoken to Chef White, and he said you were here as his runner?' he said.

Rodriguez laughed.

'His runner? Was that how he described me? Cheeky bastard,' Rodriguez said.

Moretti coughed. 'Well, those weren't his exact words, but my understanding was that you delivered any food he prepared,' he said.

'I'm trained to operate in the hospitality industry, Mr Moretti. My work can involve assisting the chef in the delivery of food, prepping said food for cooking or, if it's a salad, simple presentation. From the way you described my job, I'm no better than a drugs mule for a second-rate dealer,' she quipped.

Moretti laughed. He liked the way Rodriguez was coming across. Since he'd arrived at Heath Hall, he'd hated the stuffiness of the place and the formal tone. Rodriguez added a natural element to what Moretti considered a faked environment.

'Fair comment. When did you arrive here?'

'The same time as Derek, Mr White,' she said.

'How do you know what time Mr White arrived?'

Rodriguez frowned. 'Because we shared a taxi,' she said.

Moretti raised his eyebrows. Rodriguez continued.

'We live together, Sergeant... so we travelled together for work. I don't see anything suspicious about that arrangement, do you?' She smirked.

Moretti placed his pen down and pursed his lips. 'It would have been helpful if Mr White had mentioned this. His manner was elusive when it came to how he came to be working with you here,' he said.

Rodriguez sighed then laughed.

'Association is frowned upon by the agency that employs us. He probably didn't want to mention our link because of this. The money is good when Mr Petrov is in town. As a result, we can't afford to turn down any offer of working for him. As far as we know, he isn't aware of our domestic status. He's a man who likes to know his staff get along. He's made it known to Mrs Middleton, who arranges staffing for him, that he prefers his outside staff to be unassociated. He feels this adds to a slicker and smoother working operation. I don't see it myself, but then again, I'm not paying. He is,' she said.

Moretti nodded. He felt he was getting an honest appraisal from Rodriguez despite her forthright demeanour. In previous investigations a brash attitude was employed by a witness to deflect him from the truth but, on this occasion, he felt it was being employed to provide openness and clarity as to her situation. Domestically, at least, and how this could affect her future employment. Moretti's mind flitted to Tabatha, a neighbour of his whom he'd had a brief relationship with. She was an artist who supplemented her income stripping at a club in central London. She didn't enjoy the work, but it was good money and meant she could afford her mooring fees and engage in the art she loved to create without fear of being made homeless. Rodriguez worked where the money was, and Petrov clearly paid well.

'You took food to Mr Petrov? When was that?'

Rodriguez glanced up then back at Moretti. 'It was shortly after midnight. I'd checked. I was taking a bottled water and a towel to Mr Petrov's room, in the main house suite, not the panic room. He'd contacted Mrs Middleton about the items, and she'd asked me to fulfil the request as she was busy. Derek paged me, and I attended the kitchen and took the plate of food – steak and salad.'

'Who'd requested the food?' Moretti asked.

'Mr Petrov, allegedly.'

'Allegedly?'

'I was told to take it to Mr Petrov by Mrs Middleton. I assumed he'd made the request,' she said.

'So, you got the food and then what happened?'

'On my way there, I was intercepted by one of Mr Petrov's security team. He insisted he took the plate and dismissed me. He was near the koi pool in the lobby. I was about to climb the stairs to leave it in Mr Petrov's room,' she said.

'But you didn't know where Mr Petrov was?' Moretti said.

'That's correct. House protocol is to leave the food in the guest's main room if they don't say where they are. Unusual, I know, but some guests are strange like that. They order and move about the house, so we never know where they are. Makes things easier and we can always go and retrieve it and take it to them if they complain or let us know where they wanted it. Some change their minds too, especially if they're wasted. You know what I mean by that, Sergeant, I'm sure,' she said.

Moretti didn't reply immediately. Why would a guest order food and not say where it was to be brought? It sounded ridiculous and not a practice he'd ever used at a hotel. Not that this was a hotel, of course, and he was learning that the people who hired Heath Hall were also considered to be unique in their requirements. It didn't make sense to him at all.

'After you handed over the food, what did you do?'

'I went back to the kitchen.'

'And the guard?'

'I don't know where he went. I left him at the bottom of the stairs.'

'Who was the guard? Does he have a name?' Moretti asked.

'Not that I know. He's the one closest to Mr Petrov though. By that, I mean he's aways around him whenever I've worked here,' she said with a quick smile, as though to say there was nothing more she could add.

Moretti glanced at Nash who'd been listening, and she shook her head.

'Thank you. If I need to ask you anything else, I'll be in touch. I'm afraid you'll have to remain here while we speak to the remaining staff. Hopefully you'll be able to go home after that. Thanks for your cooperation,' Moretti said.

'So much for free to leave,' Rodriguez said, raising her eyebrows before she stood and exited the room with the same haste she'd entered it.

CHAPTER TWELVE

Nash paced the poolside. They'd returned to the now emptied pool to make sense of what happened to Harrington. Nash was troubled by the meeting with Commander Allen. It had been convened in haste for her, whereas he'd had time to deliberate what he was going to say, and no doubt had information he wasn't sharing with her. After several attempts at calling her DCI, she'd messaged his mobile only to be met with a text that said he was busy, that he was aware she'd met with Allen and to adhere to the commander's wishes.

She wasn't surprised. Her DCI's nickname was Jelly, and he was living up to his name. She was left with little option. She turned to Moretti who was squatting at the edge of the pool staring into the empty void.

'What do we know, Nick?' Moretti looked up at her then stood. He stepped back from the edge of the pool.

'Very little. The inside team are doing all they can to get the research turned around but coming up with nothing of value in terms of leads. Petrov's research is proving problematic due to the liaison with Russia and scant information held with us about his protection team or the man himself. Not that I'd expect to read anything startling. As for Harrington, her next of kin have been informed. They're in America. They requested time to assimilate what they'd been told, before making any decision about when they'd return to the UK to manage their daughter's affairs,' he said.

Nash pulled at her hair. 'Harrington was an American citizen?'

'She was born in Florida. She has US Citizenship. Moved to the UK to study politics and languages at Cambridge when she was nineteen,' Moretti said.

'We're up against the clock, Nick. Allen will shut this down if we can't present him with tangible evidence of a suspect within this building or anything that would convince him we need the scene to be preserved. I've done all I can and will continue to hold the line, but it won't be easy. Whoever killed Harrington is most likely still here. POLSA have conducted a thorough search of the gardens and grounds, and nothing has been found to assist us. No recent tracks or any other site that appears to have been disturbed where Harrington could have been killed prior to ending up in the pool. That's not to say I'm entirely convinced that she was killed elsewhere but Dr King hasn't reassured us of that yet. You've told me McNeil, the private security dog handler, was on the grounds of the estate last night and that he's not reported anyone acting suspiciously or had his dog deal with any intruder. Petrov's security is very tight. If there was an intruder then they'd have to be very skilled to infiltrate the grounds and house, commit murder then leave without a trace. The reaction of his protection team on finding Harrington was extreme. Granted, Petrov's a man of wealth, but even so, to go straight to the safe room and then have him remain there is OTT. I'm not ruling out that our suspect is long gone, but my gut's saying that's not the case.'

Moretti waited. He could see Nash wasn't done.

'I want to speak with Petrov again. Bollocks to immunity and diplomatic privilege. He's a businessman. If he's innocent, he'll talk despite any legal advice to the contrary,' she said.

Moretti shrugged. 'I'm not so confident, Pip. If we go at him again then he could up and leave and we will have few options left as we're no further forward evidentially,' he said.

Nash looked up at the ceiling and back at Moretti. 'I can't let the pressure off, Nick. Petrov must feel that the room he's in isn't a no-go zone to me or any of our team while this investigation is running. Charlotte Harrington's family need to know we are doing our utmost to establish who killed their daughter,' she said.

Moretti followed Nash out of the pool area and back towards the meeting room. Nash walked with purpose and despite his lengthy stride, Moretti struggled to keep up. As Nash entered the room, Middleton suddenly stood up. Nash stopped abruptly and Moretti narrowly missed colliding with her back.

'What are you doing in here unsupervised?' Nash said, setting a pad and pen on the desk.

'I work here, Inspector, I was passing with the intention of offering refreshment. The pool area is humid and you'd both been in there for some time,' she said.

Nash batted her eyelids. 'I appreciate the intention, but I don't appreciate you being alone in a room designated for my use. Please respect that.'

Middleton raised her eyebrows and managed a weak smile. Middleton extracted herself from the room, quietly closing the door as she left.

'Great, now I'm without coffee,' Moretti said, plonking himself into a chair.

'It would appear not,' Nash said, nodding towards a hostess trolley that had been obscured behind Middleton.

'I'll pour,' Moretti said.

He walked over to the ornate silver pot and poured. Nash operated the drop-down screen and waited for the connection with Petrov's suite to become live.

Nash sat back and watched as the screen activated and Petrov's living area filled the white. Petrov wasn't present, but one of his guards was sitting where Petrov had been previously. He twitched as the suite phone rang out. He leaned forwards and answered it.

'Yes?'

'This is DI Nash. I wish to speak with Mr Petrov.'

The male sat back and cradled the phone between his shoulder and ear. He wasn't dressed in the habitual dark suit. A faded pair of denim jeans and a black T-shirt were now part of his attire.

'He is sleeping,' the man said.

'Can I enquire as to who you are?' Nash said.

'I am his primary close protection officer,' he replied, his face devoid of emotion.

'I meant your name?' Nash said.

The bodyguard leaned forwards holding the phone to his ear. Nash noted a scar over his right eyebrow.

'You should know these things already. You're police, yes?'

Nash sighed. 'It's customary to introduce yourself in a conversation, that's all,' she said, hoping this would elicit a convivial message. She was wrong.

'I am Russian, not English. Our customs are not yours.'

Nash glanced at Moretti who had the laptop open and could only manage a shrug of support.

Nash observed the bodyguard. There was nothing about the man she could see to exploit. His body language defied interpretation. He wasn't the one she'd seen on the gate and by all accounts this was the first time she'd noticed him as part of Petrov's team of four. A mass of muscle that wasn't for shifting.

'Get Mr Petrov to the phone,' Nash said.

The bodyguard sat back and placed the phone on a low table.

'I know you can hear me. The system is designed for two-way conversations without the need of the phone. Now please let Mr Petrov know his presence is required,' Nash said, her tone clipped.

The bodyguard laughed. 'Mr Petrov is sleeping. He is not for disturbing. When he makes this request, he means it,' he said.

Nash pinched her forehead. 'OK... OK, this isn't a call that can be taken later. I'm investigating a murder. A murder where Mr Petrov, by his presence at the scene, is a key person and I will speak to him, whether it's now or in the early hours of the morning. I will continue to make contact until he decides it's the best option,' Nash said. Her gut eased as she made her wishes known. She was aware she was losing a grip on the investigation due to the control being practiced by outside agents. It wasn't something she was used to.

To her surprise, the bodyguard spoke.

'You mistake the situation. Mr Petrov has immunity in your country, as you well know. As his lead protection officer, and son, I have a duty to see that his legal rights in your country are respected,' he said.

Nash was still looking at the screen and noted that he hadn't spoken his reply to the front but had been engaging off to the side. Nash zoomed the camera out and she could see he was alone.

She focussed on her breathing to refrain from pouncing on his revelation that he was Petrov's son. She glanced across at Moretti who was engaged in a search on the computer. He coughed and she saw on his screen an image of the man who was on the main one.

'Very well. I'll be in touch,' she said, terminating the link.

Moretti mouthed as though he were about to speak, his palms raised in front as though he was cradling an invisible ball. Nash held her palms up and he relaxed his posture.

'I need him to believe I haven't heard the statement about his relationship to Petrov. Call it detective's intuition, but I think he's dropped it in as bait. For what purpose, I don't know, but I wasn't feeling comfortable taking it and getting reeled in. Not until I have some background on Petrov's family setup,' she said, joining Moretti at the table and looking at the image on his screen.

The still showed a male in his mid-twenties exiting what appeared to be a nightclub or casino. Multi-coloured lights from above illuminated his glowing face. The image appeared to have been cropped as he was holding someone's hand.

'Seems his son is a bit of a hedonist,' Moretti said, tapping a pencil against the screen where a script in Russian was presented around the photo. 'I'll get it translated. I'd rather use an interpreter than a translation app, but that's the gist of an article related to the picture,' he said.

Nash nodded. 'How did you find the image?'

'I googled Petrov and son and got a lucky hit.'

'Get a full profile and a name. I appreciate we need this translated, but we need it fast. Get Sagona on the case, he'll have contacts that can work this up. It may come to nothing, but my instinct's telling me Petrov's son isn't one for remaining mute for as long as his father,' she said.

Moretti laughed. 'So we're investigating on gut instinct now?'

Nash breathed deeply before replying, 'No. Hostage negotiation training, Nick. Active listening and taking away the message I was meant to hear.'

Moretti pursed his lips and nodded before returning to his laptop. He picked up his work mobile and called George Sagona, their incident room manager at Hendon, to brief him on his next task.

CHAPTER THIRTEEN

Moretti closed his eyes for a beat as he prepared for Dr King to return to the room. King hadn't left the side of the table where Harrington lay, but to Moretti, the doctor's mind was far from there and deep in thought as he peered over his half-moon glasses at the victim's neck. King stepped back and straightened up.

'Well, I'll be damned,' he said, leaving Moretti none the wiser.

Moretti had learned through many an occasion dealing with Dr King that it wasn't prudent to interrupt the man until he addressed the person with him in the room. The one who was alive, that is.

'Come closer, Sergeant, don't be shy,' King said.

Moretti sidled up closer to King. King circled a scalpel like a wand around an area of Harrington's neck and Moretti made a good effort at showing he was being attentive, but not at what exactly he was meant to be noting.

'Now, pay attention. As you are no doubt aware, ligature marks on the neck are subject to great variation. The marks left are all dependent on the amount of pressure used, type of restraint, and levels of resistance offered by the victim,' King said, stooping level with Harrington's neck before standing.

'I can tell you she wasn't strangled with a towel. This is important. She was found in a swimming pool after all. She was also killed before she entered the water. I can confirm this now having examined her lungs. Don't look so confused, Nicholas, there was an absence of fluid. Where was she killed? That's your job to establish, but I would expect to find some evidence of skin or hair under her nails. She would have put up a struggle, that's for sure, unless she was drugged before she was strangled. The ligature that caused these marks wasn't of a soft material either. Now, this is very important, so listen and note, the belt that was on her body *wasn't* the one that was used to strangle her,' King said, pausing to allow his revelation to hang in the stale air.

Moretti's eyes flared. He noted how King's eyebrows raised. Despite Dr King's mask, Moretti could tell King was pleased with how he had reacted.

'Well, I never. Nash won't be happy with that, not one bit,' Moretti said.

'Facts are facts, Nicholas, and Pippa will have to deal with them. Now, where was I, oh yes. So, what was used and why wasn't the belt you found the one? See here, the lines on her neck?'

Moretti leaned forwards. Two track lines stretched around Harrington's neck.

'Yes, I can see the lines. They look to me like they'd be from the belt we found,' he offered.

Dr King nodded. 'You'd be reasonable in your assumption, but we don't deal in assumptions, do we, Sergeant. We deal with facts. I can tell you the width of the mark on her neck doesn't correspond to the measurements of the belt you discovered on her body.'

King paused, and Moretti broke his own rule.

'It was planted on her; Petrov's belt?'

King raised his nose. 'I didn't say that, Sergeant. I said the belt you found on her body wasn't the ligature used to asphyxiate her,' King said, before lowering his nostrils. 'The ligature you seek is thinner than the one on her body – by a centimetre. I can tell you it's made of leather though, by the marks on her skin. I've swabbed the area to ascertain the type of tannin that's leached upon her skin. I will need to ascertain if it's from the belt we recovered or another source material. I'm studious, as you know, and keen to see this poor woman's death solved,' he said.

Moretti let out a sigh. His mask billowed briefly before it returned to its natural state. Dr King snapped off his gloves and Moretti took this as a sign they were done.

'Let's grab a drink,' King said, dropping his mask in a metallic bowl. He nodded at an attendant that he was finished, and they could take over.

They moved to King's office. It was more of a study than an administrative cube. Dark wooden bookcases lined the walls, the various academic texts separated at intervals by jars of fluid. Some held samples, others were empty. To Moretti's astonishment, King retrieved a bottle of Scotch from a drawer under a desk that wouldn't have looked out of place in Heath Hall.

'Will you join me or are you still on duty?' he said.

Moretti shrugged. 'One won't harm.'

The pathologist poured a finger of Scotch and passed Moretti his glass. King sat opposite him in a battered-looking leather tub chair and raised his feet upon a matching foot stool.

'Feel free to smoke. I treat this space as home. I'm here so often,' King said, grabbing his own pipe and tobacco.

Both men conducted their individual rituals of loading their bowls, each content in the other's company. Business had been concluded. Moretti felt a degree of relaxation he had missed in many a day. His life had been hectic over the past months, with a shift in his houseboat's moorings, and more police work than he needed. He'd taken the decision to relocate after a work-related incident had come crashing into his private life. That meant he and his neighbour Tabatha weren't in each other's pockets as much as they had been, their unsocial hours of work keeping them apart.

King was the first to complete his smoking preparations and Moretti realised he was languishing in melancholy as the room filled with a sweet scent of rum and raisin.

'I'll have the results of toxicology, stomach, neck and nail swabs turned around quickly. I understand this has political fallout too. I have a great deal of respect for your DI and your good self, Nicholas,' King said, emphasising his point with the stem of his pipe.

Moretti nodded in appreciation and lit up. 'Do you ever tire of this job?' he asked.

King pursed his lips lightly. His face became vacant. 'No,' he said, and drew in a lungful of tobacco, 'I have a duty of care to the dead and their families. One I intend to see through until I'm told I'm no longer of use, you?'

'Policing or dealing with death?'

'Both.'

Moretti's head dipped and rose, his eyes met Dr King's. 'I don't know. I struggle with the futility of what we achieve. Are we making a difference or just bowing to the demands of higher management? Investigation has become a statistical art, the human element's vanished.' He sat back.

There was a brief silence between them, one of contemplation.

'Nick, you are a young man with a fruitful career ahead of you. The wheel will always turn no matter how often it is reinvented by those who think they know best. The politics cannot change our nature, that is innate, an intrinsic part of who we are and why we do the jobs we do. Otherwise, you'd be off dealing with crime of a less invasive nature. You were meant to do this role, Nick. A calling, if you will.'

Moretti smirked. 'It was the only role available on promotion, after a year in uniform as a sergeant. A way of getting back to detective duty. In all honesty, I feel out of my depth with these investigations.'

King dipped his head and smiled. His eyes flared above his spectacles and Moretti noted his face flushed. 'Don't we all, Sergeant, don't we all. Whatever you do, Nicholas, don't let the bastards grind you down,' King said, raising his glass.

Moretti reciprocated. Both men smiled as they took a good gulp of Scotch. Moretti relished the warmth of the liquid that soothed his throat and calmed his stomach. Life was good, even in death.

CHAPTER FOURTEEN

Moretti ensured the doors to the meeting room at Heath Hall were secure. He'd scanned the room with the device Middleton had left and there'd been no change to the readings. Moretti felt it was wise, as a security measure, before he briefed Nash about what Dr King had discovered. The makeshift incident room didn't fill him with confidence that they weren't being monitored remotely.

'You're being thorough?' Nash said.

Moretti sat down alongside her. 'I thought you liked thorough,' he said, turning to her.

Nash smirked.

'Right. Here's what I learned from Dr King at the post-mortem. The belt we recovered from Harrington's body *wasn't* the one used to kill her,' he said.

Nash's eyebrows raised.

'Is that it?' he said.

'Is what it?'

'A shrug of your eyebrows. I thought you'd be a bit more... reactive.' His shoulders sank as he leaned back in his chair.

Nash smiled. 'You should know me better by now, Nick. I hadn't voiced my opinion, as it was too early, but the whole scenario we've been presented with appears staged. I couldn't put my finger on the why until now,' she said.

Moretti spied the hostess trolley; he leaned back and dragged it over. Nash shook her head when he offered her coffee, but he poured himself one.

'I get where you're coming from. It all seems too clinical. I'm used to at least some show of outward force. Seeing Harrington afloat with the belt neatly draped across her back wasn't what I expected. Not that I had any notion of what the scene would present. With these body-worn cameras uniform are using, we can see what we are about to examine and assess before we go in, but here... here is way out of my comfort zone, Pip,' he said, taking a sip of coffee.

He set his cup down. 'Dr King will have toxicology and the other samples fast-tracked. He's aware of the political interest and wants to help where he can. How quick that will be is anyone's guess.'

Moretti watched as Nash's scrawl filled a page in her daybook. He waited patiently before he continued, 'Pip, what do we do now? Do we wait for the toxicology results from Dr King or try and find the belt used to kill her?'

Nash stopped writing and set her pen down.

'What makes you think it's a belt that was used?' she said.

'Dr King said the ligature that caused the marks was thinner than the belt we found on the body,' he said.

'Nick, we must remain open-minded. He didn't say the ligature was a belt, did he? It's easy to be duped by the arena we find ourselves in. Dr King is normally very specific, but as you've just alluded, he's not saying it *must* be another belt. He's saying a ligature made of leather. That's different,' she said, picking up her pen and tapping it against her temple.

Moretti pursed his lips as he sat back, coffee cup in hand. She was right, of course, she always was. He admired the way Nash could remain open-minded where his mind could be cast adrift on a current that only headed one way.

Moretti broke their silence. 'I'll check the drapes. I've seen a few knocking about. They must have tie backs. They'd have to be robust for those floor-to-ceiling curtains. I'll get POLSA back too and have them go over the house. Let's hope they find something,' he said.

He looked at Nash who continued to tap her temple with her pen. Her eyes squeezed shut as she played a paradiddle on her head. He let her continue and he was glad he did. Her pensive countenance shifted. Her shoulders straightened as her chin raised to the ceiling, her eyes wide. Moretti noticed how the white of her eyeballs contrasted with the blue that circled her pupils. She lowered her chin and turned to face him. Her lips parted in a smile before she spoke.

'No, Nick, let's speak with John McNeil, the dog man. If anyone uses leather it's him – a good lead, Nick… see what I did there?' she said as she chuckled to herself.

Moretti let her words sink in and as they did his mind cast back to the first time he'd encountered McNeil and the leather lead that was draped over his chest and back. Inwardly he cursed himself for not seeing this earlier, but reminded himself that he couldn't have known at that stage as they thought the ligature had been recovered. McNeil had been relaxed in Moretti's company and Moretti put this down to his having been in the police prior to going freelance. He breathed in deeply and acknowledged it was better they pursued this line of enquiry now rather than discover it later.

'You're a smart cookie, ma'am,' he said.

Nash looked at him as she gathered up her daybook. 'Cookies come in packets, Nick. Task the POLSA team to search the van McNeil arrived in too,' she replied, with a warm smile.

CHAPTER FIFTEEN

Nash approached the log cabin where Moretti had last seen McNeil. She checked her watch, it showed 6 p.m. There was no light coming from the single curtained window that overlooked the garden. There was still daylight, so perhaps there was no need for the lights to be on at the cabin. Either that, or McNeil wasn't where he'd been told to remain. She'd sent Moretti to check the gardens and greenhouse area in case McNeil was walking his dog. She stepped onto the wooden veranda that skirted the front of the cabin. The boards creaked as she trod.

'Can I help you?' a voice said.

Nash turned to her left to see a male dressed in dark overalls, spaniel at his feet, tennis ball firmly in the dog's jaws.

'DI Nash – John McNeil, I presume?' she said, stepping back onto her right foot as she stood side-on to the handler.

Nash observed McNeil's eyes alter from flared to a squint, despite the sun being behind him.

'Yeah, where's the Moretti fella?' he asked.

'Behind you,' Moretti said, taking a hold of the handler's arm.

'Oi – what the fuck,' McNeil remonstrated as Moretti firmed up his grip on his arm.

Nash stepped forwards and unclipped the lead that enveloped McNeil's torso. The spaniel looked between

McNeil and Nash before scooting over to a nearby rhododendron bush.

'Look, I know the score here. You're way out of line,' McNeil said, looking for his dog who was roaming the edge of the bush, nose down. McNeil bellowed at the dog to return.

'You're ex-police? Doesn't surprise me,' Nash said.

'City police for twenty years,' McNeil said.

'Then you'll know what's coming next. You're under arrest on suspicion of murder. You don't have to say anything, but it may harm your defence if you don't mention now, something you may rely on in court. Anything you do say may be given in evidence if your case is brought to trial. We'll have your dog looked after. Let's go,' Nash said, as Moretti led McNeil towards the front of Heath Hall where a waiting police vehicle was parked, engine running.

* * *

The custody suite at Islington was buzzing. A hive of activity. Moretti waited with McNeil in a holding cage in the rear yard along with two uniform PCs, both with their own suspects for unrelated matters to Moretti's. Moretti noted McNeil's shoulders trembled despite the relative warmth of the evening.

'Handcuffs bothering you?' Moretti said, without any empathy in his voice.

McNeil bowed his head and swallowed. 'Can you move them to the front? My shoulders are shot after years hauling dogs about,' he said.

Moretti sighed. McNeil had been compliant. Moretti removed them into a front-stack, checked for tightness, and double-locked the cuffs' mechanism.

McNeil nodded his appreciation.

'How long will I be here?' he said, shuffling his feet.

'As long as it takes,' Moretti said. As soon as he spoke, they were summoned into the main custody area.

The interview room felt warm. A drier heat to that of the pool at Heath Hall. Moretti took off his jacket. He and Nash settled in before McNeil was brought to them by a gaoler.

'I've heard from Jonesy at Heath Hall. Petrov is out of his room,' Moretti said.

Nash chinned the air. 'That was quick. The efficiency of Mrs Middleton strikes again. Good luck to Jonesy and JJ dealing with her while we're here,' she said.

DC Jones and DC Jules Johnson were chosen from her squad to ensure the POLSA team were left unhindered to conduct a search of the house, van, and cabin while Nash and Moretti were at Islington. Nash had agreed with Moretti that it wouldn't harm to have the house searched in the unlikely event that the course of action she'd proposed with McNeil was incorrect. It would all add to the prosecution case. No stone left unturned.

The DCs were selected for their role at the house based on two factors: strength and the power to annoy. JJ was imposing, but a gentle giant. Jonesy was likely to have Petrov and his security team scurry back to the sanctuary of the safe room within minutes of confronting him on any issue he felt was "weary". He had a knack of making people he didn't want around, depart quickly.

McNeil was escorted into the interview room by a wiry-looking gaoler. Moretti nodded at McNeil to sit in a single seat opposite them. McNeil was happy to be interviewed without legal representation. His desire to get out of the building overcame his need to have a solicitor holding him up. Nash was happy to continue and so was Moretti. With the preamble over, Moretti began the interview while Nash observed McNeil's body language and made notes.

'Before we start, I want you both to know you've truly fucked up here. I'm innocent,' McNeil stated, leaning back in his chair. 'If I was guilty, I'd have a brief sat with me, but I've nothing to hide.'

Moretti leaned forwards and McNeil remained tilted on the legs of his chair against the wall. Moretti noted his stomach tighten and his throat had gone dry. He took a sip out of a bottle of water he'd brought in. He hadn't voiced his apprehension at Nash's eagerness to arrest McNeil first and search the property second. This aggravated him. He wished he'd spoken up before she'd waltzed him over to the cabin and made the arrest. There was also something about McNeil that troubled him. His easy-going attitude at the cabin upon his arrest being one. He'd been vociferous when Moretti had handcuffed him, but then calmed down the moment they were on. McNeil was mute in the car, content to peer out the window. Other than asking who had his dog, he was indifferent. Moretti considered that either he was a good actor or he had nothing to do with the murder. An ex-cop having no legal representation for an arrest and interview about a murder was another issue but they were way beyond that now.

'Well, we'll stop here then, shall we?' Moretti said, putting the now empty plastic water bottle in the bin.

'Suits me,' McNeil said.

'Thing is, John, you've some questions to answer. Questions I need answers to before I can see where the land lies. Answers that will determine whether you stay or go,' Moretti said, his stomach beginning to release its grip.

'Crack on,' McNeil said.

Moretti wasted no time. 'When I saw you earlier today, I asked if you'd seen anyone in the grounds, you said you hadn't.'

'Correct. So why did you take my lead? I'll tell you why, Detective, because you think I killed her with it. Good luck proving that,' McNeil said.

'Her?' Moretti said.

McNeil swallowed. 'Charlotte Harrington, the woman in the pool.'

'So, you know who died there? That wasn't my impression when we first met,' Moretti said.

'I found out who it was after you left,' he said.

'Who told you? You said you'd stay at the cabin – alone,' Moretti said.

McNeil tilted forwards in his chair until his hands connected with the edge of the desk. 'I wasn't under arrest and I was free to leave. I bumped into another staff member who will remain nameless and asked them. There's no crime in that, not the last time I looked.'

'Whose lead is the one we seized?'

'What do you think?'

'Answer the question, McNeil,' Moretti demanded.

McNeil swallowed and sighed. 'It's my lead, yes,' he said.

'Where did you get it and how long have you had it?'

'It's new. From a catalogue of dog equipment related to my work. I have a receipt at home, you know, for tax purposes,' he said, a note of sarcasm in his voice.

Moretti could tell McNeil was beginning to relax. His initial reticence had waned.

'How well did you know Charlotte Harrington?' Moretti asked.

'I didn't know her, but I knew of her. I was tasked as a dog handler, not to fraternise with the staff or guests. Bottom line is, Detectives, you're wasting your time with me. Do what you must with the lead, it's obvious you think it was involved in her death. But I didn't kill her, and I don't know who did,' he said.

'Think what you will, Mr McNeil, but as you are aware from your previous career as a police officer, we remove items that we deem may become a safety issue upon arrest. Your safety and ours,' Moretti said.

McNeil shook his head in disbelief.

Moretti glanced across at Nash who offered no help whatsoever.

'I want to go over every aspect of your time at Heath Hall. How you came to be employed there and details of your working day. That will include whom you interacted with, where and when. Agreed?'

McNeil nodded and Moretti got on with the rest of the interview while Nash made notes.

After the interview was concluded, McNeil was returned to his cell. Moretti closed the interview room door.

'Thanks for the help,' he said to Nash while she stirred a custody coffee.

'You were doing fine on your own,' she said.

'Bollocks, Pip. What do you know that I don't? You may as well have stayed at Heath Hall,' Moretti said, forearms firm across his chest.

'I can see you're pissed off. I know from the way you've been since I suggested McNeil's arrest that you weren't entirely happy with the decision. Fact is, it had to be done,' Nash said.

Moretti relaxed his arms to the table. 'Why? We could have interviewed him under caution without the need to haul him here. There's nothing to say his lead was the ligature – unless I'm missing something.'

Nash rubbed her eyes. 'Of course you're right, however because of nicking McNeil, Petrov feels safe to come out of his own luxury cell. We were right to arrest, Nick. We had other options, but there's nothing to say, at this stage, that McNeil isn't involved in Harrington's murder. Now Petrov feels free, I intend to go after him. Hopefully he'll change his mind and speak with us, rather than hide behind diplomatic immunity,' Nash said.

'I don't hold the same hope,' Moretti said as a gaoler opened the interview room door and told them McNeil wanted a tea – milk, two sugars.

CHAPTER SIXTEEN

The handover from DCs Jones and Johnson was brief. Petrov was in a wing of the main house conducting his business from there. He hadn't engaged with the detectives or hindered the POLSA team search, which had concluded their role. Two further dog leads were found in McNeil's van and removed for further forensic examination. No other potential items of evidential value were found elsewhere. The DCs left and Nash resumed control. She summoned Middleton to the meeting room via the internal phone.

'Am I to understand Mr Petrov is available to speak, now he's out of the panic room?' Nash asked.

Middleton stood in the doorway, hesitant to enter. 'No. Mr Petrov is of the same mind as before, Detective Inspector. He's asked me to convey that he hopes the investigation will be drawn to a close soon. He wishes to return home now a suspect has been arrested,' Middleton said.

Nash pressed the tip of her tongue at the crease of her lips, 'Please inform Mr Petrov that I will let him know once my investigation has concluded. Until then, I hope he enjoys the remainder of his time at Heath Hall,' Nash said. 'The swimming pool will be unavailable for some time,' she added.

Nash's mobile phone rang out and she answered.

'Nash,' she said.

'Commander Allen. What's going on at Heath Hall? Why hasn't the scene been closed?' he demanded.

Moretti ushered Middleton out of the room. Nash got up from where she'd been sitting and used the few seconds it took for her walk from chair to window to compose herself before replying.

'Sir, we have a development. A suspect's been arrested and is currently in custody awaiting further interview. Until I'm at a stage where I'm satisfied the scene can be released, I'm afraid the situation remains the same,' Nash said, holding her mobile away from her ear as Allen snorted down the line.

'Did I not make our position clear? Shut. The. Scene. Down,' he ranted across the line to be heard through the speaker by those in the room.

Nash closed her eyes for a moment and focussed on her breath before she replied, 'You made *your* position crystal clear, sir. I would have thought with the rapid change in the inquiry you'd wish to give us more time. After all, this is a murder investigation, not a traffic matter.'

'I'm afraid you leave me with no choice, Inspector. I'm removing you from the investigation and closing the scene. Mark my words, your career is over, is that clear enough?' he said and hung up.

Nash looked at her phone. She stopped the phone recording she'd initiated. She tested the recording and Allen's words leaked through the speaker.

'Crystal, sir,' Nash said to the empty room.

* * *

Moretti had thought better of remaining in the meeting room while Nash took the call, deciding to make use of the smoking room. On returning to the make-do incident room, he patted his jacket pockets to ensure he'd not left his lighter or tobacco upstairs. Nash remained by the main window, running her hand through her hair and staring pensively at the uniform PC who was on the outside of the closed gate to Heath Hall where a gaggle of reporters jostled to get a shot.

'Everything OK?' Moretti said as he approached Nash.

Nash turned and walked away from the window. 'I'm off the case, Nick. Allen called. He's thrown his teddy in the corner and expects me to pick it up as I leave,' she said.

Moretti rubbed his jaw. 'Fuck. So, when are you going? Who's taking over?' Moretti garbled.

Nash rubbed her hands together. 'You should know me better than that, Nick. I'm going nowhere, not for now anyway. Allen can wait. We've a duty of care to establish who killed Charlotte Harrington. Then he can do as he wills,' she said.

Moretti nodded slowly. This was the DI he appreciated more than any other he'd worked with. Her no-nonsense approach had her labelled by some in the command as stiff, unrelenting, but Moretti knew her better than most. She was diligent and professional and didn't suffer fools.

'Where next, ma'am?'

Nash smiled. 'Don't *ma'am* me, Nick,' she said with a smirk. 'Sit down and let's run through what we know.'

Moretti did as requested and Nash remained standing.

'We know Harrington *wasn't* killed with Petrov's belt,' she said. 'There's a possibility she was killed before she entered the water. We don't know where she was killed, why, or by whose hands. The killer would have been strong. Harrington was fit and would have struggled and we've no sign of that on her body or at the poolside.'

Nash paused, and Moretti interjected.

'Unless she was drugged. Dr King mooted the same,' he said.

'Get on to Dr King's secretary. See if the results he promised to fast-track are back,' Nash said.

Nash waited as Moretti made the call. There was a period of respite as Moretti made noises akin to listening and placed his phone on the table once he'd finished.

'Well?' Nash said.

'Traces of ketamine in Harrington's urine. King reckons enough to sedate her, not kill her. Fits with her being drugged before she was strangled,' Moretti said.

Nash began to pace the room again. To an outside observer she would've appeared to be engaged in a game of rock, paper, scissors as her hands danced in the air.

'Who has access to ketamine?' Nash asked.

Moretti inhaled as he thought. 'Anyone can get hold of that on the street,' he said, unhelpfully.

Nash stopped and faced him.

'Unless you have access to a vet,' she said, picking up her phone. Nash scrolled through her contacts and pressed the screen. She waited until a connection was made.

'Custody Islington, how can I help?'

'DI Nash – Homicide Command. I'll be back in thirty minutes to interview McNeil, cell three. Can you book a room for us. Thank you,' she said. Moretti grabbed his phone and the keys to their car.

* * *

McNeil appeared to Nash to have been reflecting on his time in custody. The creased brow had slackened, and his eyes were red as though he'd been crying. There was no mention on his custody record that he'd been in distress. He was deemed fit to interview, and that was all that mattered to Nash. Her custody clock was ticking down. At this stage she didn't wish to apply for an extension on his time limits. Nash had taken the decision to lead on this interview. With the legal requirements covered, she began.

'Mr McNeil, how well would you say you care for your dog?'

McNeil, who'd been laid-back, bolted forwards. 'Cruelty to animals now, is it? You can't pin me for murder, but you'll have a go at another equally poor charge – pathetic. I treat my animals very well. Ask my vet,' he said.

'I intend to. When was the last time you spoke with your vet?'

'Is my dog ill?'

'No. Just answer the question,' Nash said.

'I haven't taken either dog to see her for over two months, why?'

Nash scratched her eyebrow. 'What drugs do you use for the training of your spaniel?' Nash asked.

McNeil's brow furrowed as he rocked back on his chair. 'I don't. She was my dog in the police and retired with me. What is all this about?' he asked.

Nash inhaled; her chest rose and fell as she expelled air in a calm and measured manner. She considered all her options, one being to steer away from the ketamine issue and leave McNeil to stew on a brief interview to see if he chose to speak with her again. Equally, she could confront him with what she knew and take things from there. She opted for the latter. She was under pressure and despite her bravado at Allen's statement, she knew he would never back down from what he'd said.

'There were traces of a controlled drug within Harrington's body. A drug that I believe was administered prior to her death. There's no evidence to suggest that she used recreational drugs. I'm asking you, as your career has centred around drugs and out of the people at Heath Hall, you could access them most easily,' she said.

As the words spilled out, she knew they were weak, supposition at best. McNeil rubbed the bridge of his nose and shook his head.

'Look, I want to help, I really do, but you are way off the mark. Yes, I am a handler whose dog is trained to detect drugs, guns, and explosives. Yes, from my experience, I would know where to go to get drugs if that was my thing. My spaniel is used at Heath Hall for detecting them. Mr Petrov is a paranoid man. He insists the grounds and house are swept for all three before he or his staff enter the building. I haven't spoken to him about why. I only deal with Middleton. I conduct the searches and report my findings to her in the form of a statement detailing the times I searched, where, and what, if anything, I found,' he said.

'What did you find before Petrov arrived?' Nash said.

'Bliss, my spaniel, indicated a scent within a small area in a cupboard outside the kitchen,' he said.

'What was found?' Nash asked.

'There was nothing there when I looked. I can't say how long it had been there or when the substance would have been removed. A first-aid kit and a few odds and sods were the only items left. Middleton said there'd been a rock star who'd rented the place for a month and had left two days before Petrov arrived. I assume drugs were stored there. Unlikely to be anything else,' he offered, looking at Nash and then to Moretti, who kept his head down as he wrote.

'What time did you search the kitchen?' Nash asked.

'It was the last room of the house, it would have been around 6 p.m. Petrov arrived an hour later once the all-clear was given by Middleton,' he said.

'I'll need to know where your dog showed an interest. Can you draw me a plan?'

McNeil nodded. 'That's no problem, it was a small cupboard to the left of the hall that lets you access the kitchen area from outside,' he said.

Nash nodded and turned off the recording.

With McNeil back in his cell she contacted the team's SOCO and requested she attend Heath Hall. Nash wanted to be there when the SOCO arrived, and she and Moretti left to meet her. She considered taking one of the command's dogs to search, but dismissed the idea, at this stage. She'd see what Yvonne could find first, based on McNeil's information.

CHAPTER SEVENTEEN

Nash and Moretti were pensive while Yvonne, their SOCO, swabbed the shelf area of the cupboard McNeil had referred to. Preliminary tests Yvonne had conducted at the scene showed traces of a controlled drug. Nash requested the sample be analysed for ketamine as well as the standard drugs run. Nash and Moretti returned to the meeting room where she checked her decision log for inspiration. Finding none, she closed it.

Nash knew she was doing all she could in the circumstances. She noted that Moretti was busying himself at his laptop, presumably answering messages from Sagona back at Hendon. Nash had a few messages on her work phone from a DS on the intelligence desk, whose team were working on all she'd requested concerning the background of Petrov's son and the translation of the article Moretti had discovered.

She sat back in an easy chair placed near an imposing fireplace within the room. The hearth was vast, but the main burning area was empty. She was glad. It meant Middleton had stuck to her word and left the room to them. She thought over McNeil's actions and what her options were in relation to his part in her investigation. The outstanding question was whether the lead they'd seized from him matched the tannin and marks on Harrington's neck. If Harrington's skin or hair was present, then her case against McNeil was strong enough to charge. All the better. She got up and strolled over to Moretti who turned in his chair to face her.

'Get on to Sagona. Tell him to get the dynamic duo Jonesy and JJ around to search McNeil's house. They're to look for drugs. Ketamine or anything associated with it,' she said.

Moretti rubbed his eyes. Nash knew it meant he was troubled.

'Spit it out, Nick,' she said.

Moretti dropped his hands from his face where they came to rest in a loose grip on his knees. He sat forwards. 'Pip, why would he have ketamine? I'm not saying we shouldn't search his address, but the link between him being a dog owner and having access to a vet, and the ketamine is... well, a bit shit in terms of our investigative strategy. McNeil said in interview he'd know the areas to visit if he wanted drugs and that's where I'd suggest he would roam, not back to his vet,' Moretti said.

Nash stroked her chin. Moretti was right. It was weaker than a canteen tea. She knew she was clutching at straws. With Petrov hiding behind claims of diplomatic immunity, and Allen breathing down her neck, she felt pressured to throw Allen scraps of progress to keep the wolf at bay. She had little else to assist her investigation and was being led by what she could pursue. That didn't make it viable despite its appeal as an option.

'You're right. I'll be honest, Nick, this case bothers me more than it should. I'm prevented from accessing the person I need to talk to by red tape and the one we have in custody happens to use a piece of leather for work and would have been at Heath Hall when Harrington died. What do you suggest?' she said, holding cupped hands towards her sergeant.

Moretti steepled his fingers and eased his ridged forehead against the bridge of digits.

'I agree about searching McNeil's house. It would be remiss not to. If this case arrives at court, we'll be asked why we didn't, especially when we don't have the murder weapon. I'll chase up the work on the lead we seized from McNeil. At least we can establish if it was used to strangle Harrington. If it wasn't, then we're in deep shit. This was meant to be a simple case, wasn't it? Body in a pool in a house that employs tighter security than our police stations. The suspect must be here, Pip, mustn't they?' A look of angst pained his face.

'Let's hope so,' Nash replied. 'Harrington was a fit woman, Nick. She wouldn't have let someone drug her unwittingly and strangle her. There are no defensive marks on her body recorded by Dr King, none. We need the results from under her fingernails. If there's any hope of a contact trace with our suspect, it might be there. In the meantime let's get Chef White back in here. He has a few questions to answer after our chat with Rodriguez,' she said.

Moretti nodded and left to find White.

While Nash had the room to herself, she pondered what Commander Allen had meant by his threat. Not of removal from the investigation, but about her career being over. He had sway in higher management and everyone at The Yard knew he was being groomed for the main rank – Commissioner Allen. She shivered at the thought of him overseeing the organisation she loved. Loved. Maybe she was done? Had the time come when she should move on? Pastures new beyond the dead?

Her musings were interrupted by the sound of Moretti's heavy-footed stomp as he entered the meeting room and asked White to grab a seat. Nash watched White as he sat down. His collapse to the chair was tentative and Nash noted how his eyes flitted between Moretti and her as he wiped his hands on a pair of checked trousers. No food debris came off them and Nash surmised he was feeling the heat of his body.

'Everything OK?' Nash asked White.

White coughed into his sleeve before replying.

'Yes – of course, why do you ask?' he said, hastily.

'Because you appear to have had a shock,' Nash said.

White wiped his mouth with the back of his hand and began to rock in his seat. Nash mouthed "what the fuck?"

to Moretti who shrugged his shoulders as he sat next to White.

'Do you need medical help?' Nash said.

White scratched at his hair. 'No... no, I don't. Look, I know what this is about, this "little chat", DS Moretti told me. I know you've nicked McNeil and I'd rather you heard my version of events than believe what he's obviously told you, judging by the woman who was in a head-to-toe white suit in the kitchen first-aid cupboard earlier,' White said, his pale skin flushed crimson as he spoke.

'The floor's yours,' Nash said, keen to hear what was troubling White. Her stomach felt as though a samba band were warming up in anticipation of a big finale.

'The drugs in the cabinet weren't mine, I never put them there, McNeil did. I saw him at the cupboard a few days ago, all furtive and shifty. He never had his dog either. They're always a team. It looked weird, to me, anyway. I challenged him and he told me he was leaving a package there and not to touch it. He came right up to my nose and told me if I mentioned it to Middleton or anyone else, he'd get me sacked,' he said, head bowed now his confession was out.

Nash waited a beat in case White continued, but White was mute. His hang-dog appearance told her he was done – for now.

'Thank you, Derek. I'm sure that's a weight off your mind. How did you know it was drugs McNeil was leaving?' Nash said.

White looked up at Nash. 'I looked. Who wouldn't? It's technically part of *my* kitchen, an area I'm responsible for. Lo and behold here I am being questioned by police,' he said.

Nash nodded. 'What did you find, Mr White?'

White's eyes dipped to the floor and returned to the window as he spoke. 'I don't know what type of drug it was other than it was in liquid form. A small bottle, like a pill bottle. It was clear and there was a small amount of fluid in the base, about 5ml I'd say, maybe less,' he said.

'What makes you think it was a drug?' Nash asked, keen to establish why White had concluded so.

'What else would it be?'

'You tell me,' Nash said.

'OK, an assumption on my part, but why would you be so secretive and fire off threats if the package was innocent and legal?'

Nash let the question be.

'Who collected it?' she asked.

White sat back and swallowed. 'I can't say.'

'Can't or won't?' Nash said.

'I saw one of Petrov's men lurking near the hallway after I was let in. I never saw him take it, but when I went there for a butterfly strip for my finger – a knife cut – the bottle was gone. There was no one else who came into the hallway other than Camilla. She smokes out there,' he said.

'Would you recognise the man again?' Nash asked.

'It was the guy with a scar over his eyebrow,' White said, pointing at his right eye as his shoulders slumped.

Nash thought back to Petrov's son and the scar he had. A prominent mark evident to anyone who happened to meet him in the briefest of circumstances. The difficulty for Nash was he too had diplomatic immunity. To pursue him directly would be wasting her time and she knew it. If Petrov's son was a prime suspect, then she'd have to find a way to him by other means.

'Why didn't you mention this when we spoke before?'

White sighed. 'I didn't know it would be relevant to your investigation. I was taught to keep my head down and focus on my job, not to involve myself in anything unless it affected the efficiency of my kitchen. What happened in the pantry was over very quickly and didn't affect my reputation. Had McNeil tried to destroy me, as he threatened to, I would have challenged that. I may appear like I don't have a backbone, Inspector, but I don't suffer fools. Why else would I be employed in an elite establishment as this? Heath Hall doesn't employ weak-minded staff. The clients who rent this place have expectations of excellence, and I always deliver,' he said.

Nash noted a shift in White's sallow demeanour. His shoulders shot back as his chest swelled under his chef's tunic. His stare was intense and for a moment Nash felt like she was witnessing an addict during a moment of euphoria. White was right, he did have another side to him rarely seen outside of his world of cooking. Nash had met many detectives of a similar nature – quiet and unassuming until their sense of justice was triggered, then they'd become unstoppable in their pursuit of truth. This change was always reflected in their body language. Language Nash was witnessing as she observed White regulate his breathing and his shoulders and chest relax. She wondered just how angry White could become when pushed. Enough to kill? Only time and evidence would answer that question, and both were thin on the ground.

CHAPTER EIGHTEEN

The grounds of Heath Hall were illuminated with strategically placed pods of subtle and tranquil lighting designed to accent the staged planting. Moretti sat under the porch of McNeil's cabin, pipe lit, listening to a blackbird trill in the final moments of light from the bush where Bliss, McNeil's spaniel, had exited upon his arrest. He needed the break after Nash had informed him Petrov's son was out of bounds now it was confirmed he too was protected by diplomatic immunity. At least they had a name for him now, Maxim Petrov. The inside team had obtained a flight manifest as well as having had the news article translated.

The newspaper article was standard stuff. Rich man's son out clubbing gets in a confrontation with photographers. Not that the image showed any such confrontation, just a jaded-looking Maxim leaving a club holding the hand of a person unknown due to the crop of the photo. Moretti dismissed his thoughts. This was his final smoke in the stately grounds of the house. He and Nash had been given their marching orders by Commander Allen on the basis that the main forensic work had been exhausted and no one would be leaving the country without contacting Allen's office first. Not that Nash or Moretti could engage with Petrov's entourage anyway.

Moretti knew that Petrov and son were the only ones who were afforded the immunity status. Petrov's remaining security team had all given written statements, courtesy of Petrov's lawyer, that amounted to: I saw nothing, heard nothing, and couldn't be of any help. This included the one who helped Maxim Petrov remove his father from the pool area. He claimed to have been focussed entirely on Petrov senior and didn't see the body in the water due to his concentration on doing his job – getting Petrov to a place of safety. Commander Allen had received the statements, hand-delivered to New Scotland Yard, and forwarded them on to the incident room at Hendon.

Moretti chuckled to himself as he recalled Nash's face when she'd told him what Allen had arranged behind her back. Allen had effectively had statements taken over the phone in the safe room via his personal assistant. Statements that, to Moretti and Nash, amounted to nothing. They'd never stand up in court. Not the way they were obtained. Moretti blew out smoke and thought about why Allen was so keen to see the investigation completed. Why had he chosen to interfere in such a brazen way? Yes, the heat was on from above for everyone, but Moretti sensed Allen's involvement was beyond the norm for a man of his rank. He was interrupted by Middleton, who ambled into view trussed up in a dark, padded coat that stopped short of her ankles. Moretti noted she'd opted for a pair of Hunter ankle wellies rather than her heels.

'Thought I'd find you here; may I join you?' she said, without waiting on Moretti's reply.

She sat next to him on a bench seat and withdrew a slim silver cigarette case from inside the oversized quilt. Moretti's confused gaze wasn't lost on Middleton.

'It's a sitting suit, Sergeant. I'm not all haute-couture, I have a practical side. After all, it's not about the weather, or it being too hot or cold, it's about dressing appropriately for the climate,' she said, looking for her lighter as she spoke.

'Are you not too warm under there?' Moretti said.

Middleton blinked. She fixed Moretti with a stare that he'd become accustomed to, but others would find disconcerting.

'Necessary to appear as one of the garden staff,' she said.

Moretti wondered how many garden staff operated in the dark but decided not to voice his mind. Middleton clearly had a desire to speak without being overheard and observed. She'd achieved that aim.

'What's troubling you?' he asked, offering Middleton a light, which she accepted.

She held her cigarette away from her face as she spoke, her tone hushed.

'I don't wish to speak out of turn, you understand, but I was wondering whether you'd be charging John – Mr McNeil?' she said.

Moretti raised his eyebrows. He was expecting something more than a casual question that could have been posed indoors and saved her the subterfuge of dressing like an inflatable tent.

'I don't know. Why do you ask?'

Middleton looked down at her boots and back at Moretti. Despite the weak light provided by the porch lamp, Moretti noted her eyes were watery. She was a smoker and when they'd been in the smoking room in the house she hadn't reacted in the same way to the smoke. No, this was an emotional reaction that struck Moretti as significant. He'd had Middleton labelled as a person devoid of emotion. She always seemed content to display an air of dismay that clouded any other expression of mind.

She breathed in deeply then sighed. 'I've been seeing him, on and off, since he came to work here. I was hoping we might make a go of things, now I'm not so sure,' she said.

Moretti pursed his lips. He wondered what McNeil's wife would have to say of it but refrained from comment. He'd had a text message from Jonesy to say that he and JJ were in McNeil's house and his wife was being uncooperative. Despite her resistance, they'd discovered a paper file of newspaper cuttings they'd bring back to the incident room at Hendon and were continuing the search.

'Is that all?' Moretti asked, trying to be as nonchalant as he could, hoping Middleton would continue.

'I think that's a tad trite, Sergeant. I've acknowledged I've been having an affair with a murder suspect you have in custody and that's not enough?'

Moretti remained stoic. Middleton placed her cigarette in an ashtray and dug her hands deep into the pockets of her coat.

'I know you've spoken with Derek White again. I spoke to him too. I need your reassurance I'll be safe if I tell you something, Nick.'

Moretti paused mid inhale and set his pipe down on the deck alongside the ashtray. He held his hands at his knees and stared ahead. He hated these asks. The ones where he knew he may benefit from the information about to be imparted, but nevertheless could never give any assurance as to how the information would be treated until it was heard.

'I can't give you any reassurance that whatever you might be about to tell me will, or can, remain with us. This is a murder investigation, not a Catholic confessional,' Moretti said, turning to Middleton.

Middleton produced a tissue from the pocket of her coat. She dabbed at her eyes before scrunching the paper into her palms where it remained as she observed the lights of the gardens in a thousand-yard stare. Moretti noted her demeanour. It was as though she was viewing the scene for a final time. Moretti decided he needed to be a little less cold in his approach. He sensed that whatever she had to say was important and he needed to hear it. What would happen with that information after it was said was always manageable – to him, not necessarily the person disclosing it.

'You may as well tell me what's troubling you. Now I know that you were in a relationship with McNeil, and we have him in custody, your involvement in the investigation has shifted,' Moretti said.

'By mere association? There's plenty of people on this planet who've lived to regret decisions of a personal nature they've made. I appreciate this is out of the ordinary, but I'm not a seer, Sergeant,' Middleton quipped.

Moretti nodded.

Middleton shook her head. She glanced at the floor and back to Moretti. 'Derek White's worried about his job. He told you he knew McNeil was using the first-aid cupboard to store drugs. It was a one-off,' she said.

Moretti remained silent and waited for Middleton to explain. He didn't have to wait long.

'Camilla Rodriguez came to me with a bottle she'd found in the cupboard. She came to me as she knew it shouldn't be there.'

'How did she know it was there?' Moretti asked.

'They had to get a Steri-Strip for White. He'd cut his finger using a paring knife. Rodriguez saw the bottle and pocketed it. She was trying to protect White. White used to have a drug habit and she thought he'd started again as she'd seen a similar-looking bottle in his flat. The bottle in his flat contained more than the one she brought to me. She feared he'd lose his job,' she said.

'So why not ditch the bottle? Say nothing?' he said.

'Because she knows about me and John, that's why.'

'And?'

Middleton looked away from Moretti as she spoke. 'She'd seen John McNeil at the cupboard placing the bottle down. He'd left the outside door to the hall ajar. Rodriguez had been outside smoking. White confronted McNeil, and the rest I believe you know, as White has told you. I'm telling you as I'm trying to protect myself,' Middleton said.

'Protect yourself? Do you know what's in the bottle?' Moretti asked.

Middleton swallowed. 'No. But I'd already seen the bottle in the cabin with John before Mr Petrov arrived. When I came out, John had left. I noticed the bottle had gone from the top of the bedside cabinet.'

'You noticed an innocuous bottle had gone? This all sounds very farfetched,' Moretti said.

Middleton's eyes widened. 'In my line of work there's a place for everything and everything has a place. If I see something out of its environment, I note it. Call it an occupational hazard, if you will, but that's my explanation. I meant to ask John what was in the bottle as it was unusual to see. I thought his dog may have been ill, but I didn't get the chance to ask, as events took over,' she said.

'So, Rodriguez brought it to your attention because…?'

'Because she wanted to protect White, and she knew about myself and McNeil. Her way of letting me know she knew. If I had the liquid analysed, privately, and it turned out to be an illegal substance I could sack them both. The last chef was dismissed for substance misuse after he was found snorting a trail of white powder in a staff toilet. It was John who found him. I'm aware the job comes with its pressures, but that sort of thing should happen outside Heath Hall, if you're staff,' she said.

Moretti picked up his pipe. The tobacco was cold and spent.

'What did you do with the bottle?'

'I told Rodriguez to put it back in the first-aid cupboard and I told John,' Middleton said.

'What did McNeil say?'

'He said he'd deal with it. I didn't ask him anything else and I certainly didn't want to handle it,' she said.

'Deal with it… What did you take that to mean?'

Middleton paused. Despite the thickness of her coat, the fabric rose and fell for a beat. 'I think we both know what I mean, Sergeant. He'd dispose of it.'

'Describe the bottle you saw in the cabin McNeil uses.'

'It was small; clear glass. Full, it would have held about 3-5mls of liquid. It looked to be a quarter full to me. I'm guessing though,' she said.

'And what would happen to Derek White and Camilla Rodriguez?'

'I don't understand the question,' Middleton said.

Moretti pondered just how much he should say, but with time ticking away they needed answers. Answers to motive and means among the primary ones.

'White felt that McNeil was threatening him should he disclose anything about the bottle in the cupboard. Now you've told me that you were aware of it, McNeil would be angry with White and Rodriguez, wouldn't he? You would have to sack them all, but of course, you couldn't do that as any one of them could implicate you in it,' Moretti said.

Middleton gave a brief laugh of derision. 'Sergeant, if for one minute you think my word would be secondary to a cook, his lackey, or a dog handler, you're deluded. My unblemished reputation could withstand a tornado. John McNeil may be a bit rough round the edges but he's not a violent man. Not that I've ever witnessed. Both professionally and personally. I'm not saying he wouldn't use force in his role here, but only if the circumstances required it. White could be lying, Sergeant; have you considered that?'

'We're not done. I'm waiting on some lab results, and we may need to talk again,' Moretti said.

'You know where to find me,' Middleton replied as she stood and shuffled off the deck.

Moretti watched Middleton walk back towards the house. The coat swayed as she strutted with the air of a model who'd dominated the runway at Paris Fashion Week. Moretti wondered how someone like her could find anything about McNeil remotely attractive. He wasn't an unattractive man, in terms of his features, but his lifestyle and place in society would, to Moretti, place him in a different league to Middleton, with little chance of promotion. It was certainly not a level playing field, but Moretti knew that Middleton was no fool. There had to be some advantage to her, surely. What that could possibly be, he had no idea. He was hoping Nash could come up with a theory. He left the cabin to find her and relay the latest news.

CHAPTER NINETEEN

'Again, what has this got to do with me?' McNeil said as he shifted in his seat.

The interview room felt stuffier than a Build-A-Bear convention and Moretti looked tired of McNeil's propensity to deny all knowledge when it came to the investigation. Nash had taken the information and run with it. All the way to Islington custody suite.

'Look, John, you can deny all you like, but I have it on good authority that you were in possession of a bottle that contained liquid ketamine. Where is it?' Moretti said.

'Who told you? That bitch Middleton, I suppose?'

Moretti remained focussed on McNeil's face. 'This is your opportunity to tell me what you were doing in that cupboard, John. A cupboard *you* told us you were present at as part of *your* work. A cupboard where *your* dog indicated drugs had been stored. Drugs, I hasten to add, that were in a sealed container, so I'm struggling to see how the dog picked up any scent,' Moretti said.

'Well, that shows how little you know about working with a drug detection dog,' McNeil replied.

'Enlighten me,' Moretti said.

McNeil wiped his mouth and looked away from both Moretti and Nash, who was sitting alongside her sergeant.

McNeil appeared as though he was done with talk until he broke the silence. 'What guarantees do I have if I talk?' he said.

Moretti looked to Nash and she picked up on his eye signal that this was her domain and not his.

'This is a murder investigation,' she said. 'We are asking you to account for a missing bottle that we believe contained the drug ketamine. A drug discovered within Charlotte Harrington's blood. You said your dog indicated a drug had been present at the location you provided to us. I can confirm that swabs taken by our SOCO show traces of ketamine. A jury may draw an inference from your failure to account for this bottle. A bottle, of a similar appearance, was seen by a witness in the cabin you operate from in the grounds of Heath Hall. A space that would appear to be solely for your use. You're right, Mrs Middleton saw a bottle in your room. A bottle she thought was odd, out of place. A similar bottle was brought to her by another staff member from the first-aid cupboard. A bottle that you were seen to place there. Who was the bottle for?' Nash asked.

McNeil flopped forwards, his head dropped, then he sat back and raised and dropped his arms.

'I can't believe Middleton grassed me up.'

'This is a murder inquiry, John. She's done the right thing by talking to us, and now it's your turn,' Nash said.

McNeil moaned. He scraped the palms of his hands down his face before drumming the lip of the table that separated him from the detectives. Nash let him have time to compose himself. She sensed a confession. After many years of interviewing suspects, she had a sixth sense for when a person was ready to break.

'I was asked to get hold of some ketamine by one of Petrov's security team, the big lump who was at the gate when I arrived. He said he would pay me well. He told me to leave it in the usual place, and that's what I did. White challenged me and I told him to do one – none of his business and don't worry about it. He didn't listen. I feared for my job, so I threatened him. I didn't kill that woman though; I want to make that clear. I supplied drugs, yes, but I'm no murderer. If I knew who killed her, I'd tell you, as I can see how it looks for me, what with the ligature you think is my dog lead, and now this,' he said.

'Where did you get the ketamine?' Nash said.

'If I told you that, I'd be putting my family at risk. I'm not prepared to say,' McNeil said.

Nash leaned forwards, forearms on the desk, hands clasped together. 'You better start thinking about what else you haven't said. Let me make it plain, McNeil: we have a murder victim killed with a ligature that could fit with a lead you use, a drug found in her system you acknowledge to have supplied to a bodyguard of Petrov. A bodyguard who we can't question because of diplomatic immunity. All of Petrov's security, bar one, have provided bland statements that amount to seeing and doing nothing. Unless you can come up with something that will assist my team, then I may be left with no other option than to request to the CPS that you are charged with the murder of Charlotte Harrington. You'll be remanded in custody until trial. Is that what you want?' Nash said.

McNeil looked at Moretti then back at Nash. 'I'd like to return to my cell,' he said, his face pale.

'One more question. Did you go back to the cupboard after you'd confronted White?' Nash asked.

McNeil's Adam's apple bobbed. 'Yes. The bottle was gone, I never took it, and I don't know who did or where it went,' he said.

Nash nodded and Moretti turned off the recording.

Once they were alone in the interview room, Nash turned to Moretti. 'We need evidence, Nick, and fast,' she said.

Moretti glanced at the recorder; it was off. Nash was reluctant to speak openly in a room with any recorder present when it wasn't official.

'We're doing all we can with what we have,' he said.

'It's not enough, Nick. Every time I turn my phone on there's another text from Allen demanding an update and asking when I'm leaving the house. It's not enough that he wants the scene at Heath Hall closed and us gone, he still expects results. I know the scene has been examined, but that isn't enough. The people, or person, who killed Harrington may still be there,' she said.

'So, you're ruling McNeil out?' Moretti asked.

'No. I'm keeping all options open. Having McNeil in a cell means he's contained. I believe this has caused others to come forward because of their desire to protect themselves. It's all well and good, but it's Petrov and son I need to break. I can't do that directly. Any update from Dr King?' she said.

Moretti turned his phone on and waited. A pointless exercise as there was never any signal in the custody area.

'Let's get back to Hendon and check how things are there. I'll have a signal once we're out of here,' he said.

Nash nodded and they left.

* * *

As they turned left out of Islington police station's yard, Moretti's phone pinged with a message alert. Nash was driving so he checked the screen to see a message from Jonesy.

'Nothing from Dr King, yet, but I've just had something from Jonesy,' Moretti said.

'Well?' Nash said, stopping at a set of lights.

'Holy shit,' Moretti said.

Nash shot a look at Moretti whose brow was creased as he read what appeared like an essay on his screen. She pulled over.

'What's going on?' she said, killing the engine.

Moretti handed her his phone as he spoke. 'The search is over at McNeil's, but that's not the main part. There's a request from Commander Allen to see all exhibits taken from the search. Jonesy wants to know what he should do?' Moretti said.

Nash was listening as she read the screen. She handed Moretti's phone back and took out her own. She scrolled down to Jonesy's number and called him.

'Hi Pip,' he said.

'Jonesy, what did you find at McNeil's house?' she said.

'Not a lot. There was a blue folder that contained paperwork on private security work he'd been doing, and cuttings from Russian papers and we seized some empty medical-looking bottles, ones with sealable caps. No drugs. His spaniel arrived back while I was there, courtesy of your arrangements. His black Lab went mental on seeing her. Funny things, dogs,' he said.

'Does Allen know what you have from the search?' Nash asked.

'No. His PA made the request. I thought I'd check with Nick first, see if you were aware. It's not every day the commander wants to examine our exhibits,' he said.

'I'll take the exhibits. I'll meet you outside Tintagel House in Vauxhall and take them from there,' she said.

Jonesy agreed and hung up.

'The plot thickens,' Moretti said as Nash put her phone down.

'Indeed, it does,' she said, performing a U-turn and headed towards the city.

'Allen can't have the exhibits. There needs to be a robust trail from the scene to our secure cage at the incident room. I'll be damned if I'm going to have any one of us stood in court explaining the detour to NSY. Shows how naive Allen is around investigating crime.'

Moretti gripped the coat holder near the ceiling of the car as Nash threw their vehicle through the London traffic. The inquiry was beginning to go from simmer to boil.

CHAPTER TWENTY

Nash shut the boot to their pool car before returning to the driver's seat. Jonesy and JJ had been waiting tentatively when she and Moretti arrived, keen to dump the exhibits bags and beat a hasty retreat to the sanctuary of their incident room at Hendon. Nash noted that the pharmaceutical bottles were in a clear exhibit bag. They were all like those described by Middleton and McNeil. Not that the bottles discovered at McNeil's place took Nash and her team any further forward in terms of her investigation.

There was a blue card folder which Jonesy said contained Russian newspaper articles and a few photos. They'd seized the folder as they were aware of Moretti's interest, particularly pertaining to the Russian translation he'd requested after his find on the internet in relation to Maxim Petrov. Nash decided it would be prudent to visit Claridge's. Not for dinner, but to establish when Petrov arrived and whether he had company. It was pointless going back to Heath Hall. Commander Allen had been on the phone to his counterpart in the Diplomatic Protection Group and she'd agreed to provide extra overt security for Heath Hall. Armed officers were deployed at strategic points around the perimeter of the estate and Nash deemed her scene to be secure as a result.

Not that it mattered. As far as she was concerned it was Allen's scene now. His to look after. She'd been left with no choice – leave, or be evicted. She'd had messages from other DIs on various homicide teams who offered sympathy at her predicament. Some were less supportive and claimed they'd never have been treated the way she had. Then again, they'd never had to investigate under the circumstances she'd been presented with. Nothing surprised her where the police and management were concerned. Not anymore.

Traffic across Westminster Bridge was light. They made good time to Brook Street in the heart of Mayfair. Nash found a side street, close to the venue, and parked up. As they arrived on foot, they were greeted by a plethora of national flags that swayed in the breeze upon poles that jutted out from the building. Each piece of patriotic fabric rippled in triumph above a platform that concertinaed across the frontage of the hotel. The ornate dormer provided cover for those moments of inclement London weather. Patrons were being helped from their vehicles by a gaggle of top-hatted staff in morning dress. As Nash and Moretti approached the main door, a concierge swiftly stepped forwards and opened it, beckoning the pair in with a white-gloved hand. Moretti gasped 'wow' as they stepped into the black and white floored reception.

'You can keep Heath Hall, Pip. This is my kind of place,' Moretti said, gazing around the glamour of the hotel lobby. Cream pillars dominated between white walls and chequered floor. Mirrors within bold frames reflected the opulence of the 1920s building.

Nash left Moretti to admire a vast glass sculpture that hung from the ceiling like a chandelier. She stepped up to a reception area where a female member of staff beamed at her before enquiring how she may be of assistance.

Nash looked to her side before displaying her warrant card discreetly on the desk.

'I'd like to see the booking lists for the various restaurants for last night,' Nash said.

The girl on the desk was in her early twenties. Nash found herself mesmerised by the receptionist's perfectly made-up face. In particular, the mascara enhanced her eyes of cobalt blue. They stared back at Nash with an air of defiance.

'That won't be possible, madam. They are a private record, for the hotel, and not for public consumption,' she said in a way Nash felt was a direct quote from a staff training guide or the Middleton School of Heath Hall Etiquette.

Nash placed her hands on the rim of the reception podium. 'I'm a detective inspector with the Metropolitan Police, not a member of the public with doubts about the fidelity of their spouse and an inquisitive mind. I'm asking, reasonably, to see the entries for one evening, not the entire week, month, or dining year. I will be quick, unobtrusive, and away from here within thirty minutes, unless you choose otherwise. Then I'll have my sergeant obtain a warrant. If we go down that route, it will be crystal clear to those in attendance this evening that the hotel is subject to a police search. Your choice,' she said.

The receptionist coughed into the crutch of her elbow. 'Excuse me for one moment. I'll speak with my manager,' she said, before leaving Nash and Moretti in the lobby.

'All going well I hear,' Moretti said, smiling as Nash joined him. Moretti reclined in a brown leather tub chair, legs outstretched, arms clasped behind his neck.

'Comfy, are we?' Nash remarked, choosing to stand.

Moretti seemed to note Nash's body language and extracted himself from the comfort the lobby chair provided.

'Sorry, I've never been in a posh hotel,' he said.

'Strip the chintz away and you'll discover the staff keeping it alive are no different to you and me,' Nash said.

As they looked across the lobby, a tall grey-suited swarthy-looking gentleman approached them. He had swept-back dark hair and a tan that could only have come from a machine or bottle.

'Good evening, I'm to understand you need some assistance and I may be of help. Do follow me,' he said to Nash.

Nash nodded and both she and Moretti followed the man, who strode away towards a door that he deftly unlocked with a keycard. Once they were out of view of the public, the man's rigid shoulders slumped.

'Benjamin Johansen, dining manager, at your service. I understand you need to see a record of the bookings for our restaurants for last night. They are all on computer. It would be easier and more efficient for me if you could supply me with a name with which to search,' he said.

Nash stepped closer to the screen Johansen was now poised over.

'Petrov,' she said.

Johansen typed the name and pressed send. The action elicited no return of anyone with that name. Nash wondered if Petrov had made some calls while he was ensconced in his panic suite and had all the records erased. She dismissed the notion.

'Try Harrington,' she said.

Johansen typed and again it came up blank.

'Now look, this is beginning to feel like a fishing expedition, Detective,' he said, lips tight after he spoke.

Moretti piped up. 'Try Middleton,' he said.

'This must be the last one,' Johansen said, typing in the name.

This time there was a hit. Not just for a table but for the Foyer Private Dining Room. A room that could seat ten to twenty people.

'Can you tell me when that booking was made?' Nash asked.

Johansen checked the screen. 'A month ago. I took the booking myself from a Mrs Middleton at Heath Hall. I remember because I had to move mountains to accommodate the request with such short notice for the private space. Heath Hall is a valued client, so it was my pleasure,' he added.

'Do you know who dined here last night?' Nash asked.

Johansen's eyes flashed to check his manicured nails, before returning to focus on Nash. 'The guests were Russian. All men, apart from one woman. Between us, Inspector, I wouldn't want them back,' he said, leaning in conspiratorially.

'Why?' Nash said, moving her head back.

'The intrusion in the kitchen was most unrefined. Clearly a member of the party was an important man. I believe the woman to be, let me say, his close companion. Then there were others who treated the room like a cell. Guards on doors and one insisted on being present whenever food was brought through,' he said, dropping his hands as he appeared to relax.

'Would you recognise them again?' Nash said.

'Good Lord, they aren't criminals, are they?' Johansen said, perplexed.

'You've done nothing wrong, Benjamin, but it would be helpful to me if you could have a look at some photos,' Nash said, taking her phone from her bag and accessing the HOLMES app.

She located a series of images. One was of Alex Petrov, one of Maxim Petrov and the other of Charlotte Harrington, all obtained through her inside team's research. She scrolled through, displaying the pictures to Johansen who paid enough attention to each image. Nash noted how he nodded as though he wished to see the next picture. Once she'd ran through them all, she closed the phone.

'They were all here. The one with the scar over his eye was the man interested in the kitchen and food transfer,' he said.

'Would you know what they ate?' Nash said.

Johansen thought for a moment. 'The host and his female companion picked at the menu, but the goons made sure they made up for it,' Johansen said, with a look of pride at using the word "goons" with Nash.

'Thank you, you've been most helpful,' Nash said.

'Is that all, Inspector? I could find a table for you both should you wish to dine this evening?' he said.

Moretti began to rub his palms together but Nash soon quashed his enthusiasm.

'Very kind of you, but I'm afraid murder calls,' she said.

Johansen dipped his head and with a show of his hand towards the door they'd entered by, he led them both out of the building.

CHAPTER TWENTY-ONE

Nash and Moretti sat in the car and Nash mulled over the conversation with Johansen. Clearly, Alex Petrov and Charlotte Harrington were closer than mere business associates or employer and employee. A revelation that Nash found intriguing. Middleton had given no indication that Petrov and Harrington were that close at all. She'd suggested Harrington was the object of unwanted attention, feelings she did not reciprocate. Harrington had been described as amiable by White, and McNeil was only aware that she worked there when Petrov was in the UK and McNeil was booked for his role as dog man.

She turned to Moretti who was sat scrolling through his phone with a dour expression.

'What did you make of that?' she said, wishing to hear Moretti's opinion rather than foisting hers upon him.

'I might see if Tabatha fancied lunch there, now that we can't eat thanks to your stoic desire to work,' he said.

Nash frowned. 'About what Johansen said, not your love life and sudden desire for the high life.' A hint of a smile graced her cheeks.

'Killjoy. I thought it odd that Harrington and Petrov were alone there. I appreciate they had the Men in Black with them, but all the same, what were they there to discuss? I thought she was his interpreter slash assistant for whom he was here to see, not a hire for dinner,' he offered.

'Exactly. What was the purpose? A meal planned a month ago by all accounts and a booking not organised by Petrov, but by Middleton,' Nash said.

'Petrov wouldn't conduct his own life plans, would he? When it comes to where to eat, I mean,' Moretti said, his concentration now on Nash and not on his phone.

'I'm not so sure, Nick. He's a control freak. Do you remember Middleton saying how he insisted he had his own background checks conducted on all staff at Heath Hall? That doesn't sound like a man who lives easily. Sounds like a guy perpetually in a state of fight or flight. Then there is all the theatre with him being removed to the safe room on "discovering" Harrington's body. If he was intimately involved with her, and hadn't killed her, then you'd expect him to want to help, not hinder us by hiding behind a wall of red tape,' she said.

'He had been at the Russian embassy before the meal, so maybe he knew he'd need to eat, and it would just be the two of them and his security team? Planned ahead?' he said.

Nash rubbed the bridge of her nose as she thought.

'How do we know he was at the embassy?' she said.

'We have CCTV of Petrov's car leaving the airport when he arrived in the UK. We checked the cameras that cover 6-7 Kensington Palace Gardens. His car is seen to pull up there within a reasonable timeframe of travel from the airport. Petrov is seen getting out of the car,' Moretti said.

'Was he caught on camera entering the building?' she said.

A silence from Moretti told Nash the answer before he opened his mouth to reply.

'No,' he said, sheepishly.

'So where did he go, Nick?' Nash said, swivelling in her.

'I'll need to get back to you on that,' he said, picking up his phone.

Nash noted the name Sagona being called up on the Signal app. Moretti's thumbs flashed away before he pressed his screen and placed the phone down.

'Shouldn't be too long,' he said, staring straight ahead, eyes darting to Nash before returning to the outside world.

'We need to search Harrington's home address, Nick. The focus has been Heath Hall, but it can't wait any longer,' she said.

'How about now?' Moretti said.

Nash licked her lips. 'Get the address from Sagona. Tell Jonesy to check Harrington's personal property. See if there's any keys. If not, tell him to bring the enforcer and JJ,' she said.

Moretti picked up his phone and dialled the office number.

CHAPTER TWENTY-TWO

A uniform PC watched, inquisitively, as Moretti and Nash donned their forensic suits. They'd needed no key, or enforcer, thanks to Harrington's door already being open. Open due to being forced by person or persons unknown. Prior to them attending to search, research into Harrington's address discovered a computer-aided dispatch report had been filed in relation to the property. The record had been created on the night of Harrington's murder and referred to a disturbance outside her home. Police hadn't attended, however. It was too busy, and the incident had been graded as non-urgent. The caller was a number unknown. A passer-by. A full shift cycle had been and gone before someone was finally sent to the area. The officer was diligent enough to get out of their car to check the property, where they discovered a front door ajar and the lock damaged. The PC had searched the flat and found it to be vacant. She'd told Nash it was a mess and looked like a burglary had occurred. Nash listened. Considering Harrington's death, she decided she and Moretti would wear barrier clothing.

She was glad she had. On entering Harrington's ground floor flat it was apparent that no stone had been left unturned. Nash and Moretti chose to approach as they would a murder scene. Nash was conscious of not knowing where Harrington had been killed prior to her floating in the swimming pool. She knew Harrington hadn't been moved any distance judging by her body's lividity, but she still had to establish where she was killed so she treated Harrington's flat as a possible venue, even though she knew this was a stretch too far. Why

Harrington's flat had been ransacked was a concern. It was unusual to have a body in one place and the victim's home with signs of forced entry. Nash was used to finding the body within the dwelling where the victim lived, unless it was an outdoor scene.

There was nothing known about Harrington that suggested she had any criminal connections or that she'd upset someone enough to warrant having her flat turned over and herself murdered. As Nash made her way through the rooms she noted how, although furniture had been disrupted, there was an absence of any personal effects on the floor. Where she expected to find pictures, or ornaments, there were none. It all felt very clinical. There was nothing about the place that spoke of who Harrington was as a person. There were no books nor a music collection in any physical form. Nash usually liked to see such things to get an idea of the person the victim was, but there was nothing here that would indicate Harrington's interests.

Nash felt as though Harrington had been visited by bailiffs who'd taken all that they could sell, leaving a mess to be cleared up.

'I've found where her computer was,' Moretti said, breaking Nash's concentration.

Nash left the living room. She moved through the hallway where she found Moretti framing the doorway to a small box room. Moretti moved aside to give her an unobstructed view of the room. The contents of the space consisted of a standing desk and a bookcase that was as sparse as the whitewashed walls.

'Where's the computer?' Nash said.

Moretti nodded at a lead that trailed to the floor from the desk. 'It was here, but judging by this, it's gone. Taken in the burglary?'

Nash's face cover billowed like a boat sail as she exhaled. 'I'm not so sure this is a burglary, Nick. Yes, there's been forced entry, but the trashing of the place looks staged to me. It's too organised to be done by a thief. The place feels like a safe house we'd use for a witness protection job. Not a place a woman of Harrington's standing would consider a home,' she said.

Moretti nodded. 'She was renting the place. I'll have one of the inside team make enquiries with the letting agents. Establish how long she's been here and whether there have been any concerns about her as a tenant,' he said.

Nash agreed. She moved away from the door to the room and followed the same route she'd used back to the flat's front door. She needed space to re-establish where she was in the inquiry as well as where she needed to be. She tried to ignore her internal voice, fuelled by condescension thanks to the words of Commander Allen. She desired to focus on what she knew at this stage and not on the whims of her boss. She closed her eyes for a beat and concentrated on what they'd established: Harrington hadn't drowned, she'd been asphyxiated by an implement unknown. Where this had taken place was unclear, but Harrington had ingested ketamine. When, how, and by whom it was administered remained a mystery.

Harrington had no history of drug use from the limited research that had taken place so far. Harrington's associates were limited, and she didn't use social media. They'd also been unable to find any mobile phone that was registered to her. Nash mused on this. Aside from the badge attached to Harrington's jacket there'd been no other personal property of hers found at Heath Hall. Surely, she would carry a handbag or case of some sort if she was there to assist Petrov professionally? Did she have a space at Heath Hall that was hers to store personal effects when she was there? Middleton hadn't mentioned one. Maybe not? Nash cast her mind back to the pool area and the cleanliness of the zones that were accommodated by loungers, small drinks tables and little else. Take

Harrington away, and you were looking at a pool area fit for any guest. Minimalist in furnishings, but luxurious. The changing area for guests was comfortable and practical but lacked any locked storage for personal belongings. After all, they weren't required. It wasn't open to the public. Harrington was seconded by Petrov whenever he came to the UK, so she had no office to speak of either at Heath Hall.

Someone had gone to great lengths to make the scene suspicious yet clean, and Nash needed to know why. The assailant could have drugged Harrington, waited until they thought she was unconscious, then strangled her and pushed her into the pool to make it look like she'd drowned. But why then leave the belt around her neck? Why not leave her floating face down in the water with no ligature? Any initial response by police could result in a mistaken belief it wasn't suspicious. One element that would sow doubt on it being accidental was the ligature, and the fact Harrington was dressed in her work suit. The fact there was no blood raised questions about the idea that she'd slipped, hit her head on the edge of the pool, fallen in and drowned. All supposition, of course, as there would be head injuries that Harrington doesn't have. By the time any post-mortem concluded there were drugs in Harrington's system, the crime scene would have been contaminated by other guests using the house. Nash didn't know enough about Charlotte Harrington. Her lifestyle was a mystery. Petrov was hiding behind his diplomatic status and Nash needed to break this wall down using facts not force. Facts about Harrington and how her links with Petrov went deeper than mere professional association.

There was also the question of McNeil's custody time. He was safe for Nash for another forty-eight hours. She was confident any custody reviews would see the investigation was being conducted diligently and the need for him to remain in custody was lawful, proportionate, and necessary. She sensed a tension in her stomach. She'd acted quickly in his arrest and was acutely aware that the evidence against him for Harrington's murder was weaker than an asthmatic kitten. McNeil had admitted supplying a controlled drug, so she still had that to fall back on if it came to a charge. But it was not the result she wanted for this case. She wanted Harrington's killer charged with murder. Discovering who that was, was becoming a trial in itself.

CHAPTER TWENTY-THREE

Moretti rubbed his eyes before adjusting the tilt of his laptop's screen. They'd arrived back at Heath Hall after Yvonne, their SOCO, had left Harrington's flat. Preliminary findings were slim, and Moretti wondered whether they'd ever solve this case, or if it would become another that remained open, unsolved. The evidence here was paper thin. Attributing it to a person, with confidence, looked evermore doubtful in his mind. Moretti sensed their suspect was cleverer than the average murderer they encountered at street level. He shrugged off his angst and opened a message from Sagona, their incident room manager back at Hendon.

Moretti skimmed over the opening paragraph, an opportunity Sagona had used to moan about remote working a murder investigation, until he found the main points of the update. Dr King had sent his toxicology update detailing Harrington's blood work and nail samples. Her bloods showed no presence of alcohol and drugs, prescription or otherwise. There was no evidence of any foreign debris under her nails. This would suggest she'd been unable to defend herself. Moretti sat back and ruffled his hair. He leaned in again to make sure he'd read the section correctly. Once he'd satisfied his mind that his sight wasn't deceiving him, he continued. Where were the traces of ketamine found in Harrington's body? Had they put this to McNeil under false pretences? Moretti slugged some tepid coffee to alleviate a sudden pulsing sensation that had manifested at his temples.

Her stomach contents showed she'd eaten steak and salad prior to her death. Finally, Moretti found what he needed to see, and his blood pressure lowered along with the tension in his head. Harrington's urine analysis showed traces of ketamine. Dr King concluded the amount would have been enough to cause Harrington to lose consciousness, but not enough to stop her heart.

As Moretti considered the report and Dr King's findings, Nash entered, having taken a call from Dr King prior to her return to the meeting room. She sat in a chair alongside Moretti where she began to read over his shoulder.

'Interesting about where the ketamine was found,' she said.

Moretti closed the laptop lid. 'So, you've read the report? You may as well let me know what's useful,' he said.

Nash stood and walked to the coffee pot where she poured for them both. 'I've just got off the phone to Dr King. What the analysis shows is that the drug, ketamine, had time to move from her blood to her urine. King is saying the timing fits with Harrington ingesting the drug here, at Heath Hall. Dr King's analysis of Harrington's blood and urine samples fits with the contents of the bottle McNeil admits to supplying. Our chances of talking to the guard on Petrov's team, whom McNeil says he got the drug for, are weak. We have no access to Petrov's team. McNeil knows this and could be covering his tracks behind their wall of immunity. The amount White described as being in the bottle he saw fits with the effect it must have had on Harrington when she consumed it.'

She returned with the two mugs, placing them on the table before she sat.

'It doesn't make McNeil our killer though,' Moretti said.

'It doesn't rule him out. How did the ketamine get into Harrington is the main question. I doubt she'd sit back and be injected, and Dr King isn't indicating that he found any puncture wound on her body,' Nash said.

'Unless she trusted the person?' Moretti said.

Nash shook her head.

'She doesn't drink, by all accounts, so our suspect could hardly disguise it in alcohol. There was no booze in her flat and nothing in her bloods. The other option is that it was concealed in her food. Her stomach contents fit with the meal prepared by White when she and Petrov were here. That brings White, Rodriguez, Petrov, and his son into play. They all had access to the food and drug prior to her death. But where's the motive? Why Harrington?' Nash said.

'Anything else?' Moretti asked, ignoring the question of motive. He hadn't a clue, at this stage, as to why Harrington was their victim.

Nash took a sip of coffee and exhaled through her nose.

'There is one other thing Dr King told me over the phone. He found a single dark hair at the nape of Harrington's neck. He found it odd as it's in stark contrast to her natural hair colour. Needless to say, it isn't hers. Dr King's initial thoughts from the limited work he's done on the strand is that he suspects it's from an animal. He's sent it to a forensic vet for further examination. We're certain Harrington didn't have any pets?'

Moretti shook his head. 'You saw her flat. There was no trace of any pet food, litter tray or feed bowls in the place. She doesn't strike me as the caring type, but I may be doing her a disservice making that judgement based on the spartan contents of her flat,' Moretti said.

Nash frowned. 'You could say the same of mine, Nick, but that doesn't make me uncaring, just incredibly busy and unable to find space for anyone else or anything else in my life,' she said. Her cheeks flushed as she realised how strongly she'd reacted to Moretti's off-the-cuff comment.

Moretti raised his palms. 'I wasn't suggesting anything, Pip. I was thinking of my own place. If someone analysed that, they'd say the owner was an alcoholic musician who had aspirations of freedom, the only thing tied down being the boat they lived on.'

Moretti smirked, and Nash cracked a smile.

'This job, eh, Nick?'

Moretti shrugged. 'I love it, Pip. What I don't enjoy is not making progress for those that can no longer speak,' he said.

Nash lifted her coffee cup and went to sip from it. She didn't, but used the object as a shield while she thought about what Moretti had said. Since her grilling with Commander Allen, she'd come to see her role as a part in a poorly scripted play, one where Allen was intent on shouting lines from the prompt corner, stage left. Lines Nash knew by rote. She was tired of those in ivory towers with no experience of her world crashing in and rearranging the furniture.

'Where is Alex Petrov now?' she said.

'He's in his safe room. Middleton drifted in here while you were on the phone. She informed me she'd be unavailable for a while as she was taking some supplies to him,' Moretti said.

'Supplies? What supplies and how long is he expecting to stay there?'

'No idea. How do we get him to open up to talk, Pip?'

Nash set her cup down on the table. 'We don't. We must do this the hard way, Nick. We need evidence against him and fast,' she said.

Moretti sighed.

'All the evidence we have is pointing away from Alex Petrov and onto John McNeil. McNeil had direct access to the ketamine, and we have a witness, of sorts: White can place him where he says the bottle was left. Middleton can also say she saw a similar-looking bottle on the cabin McNeil uses. With the same drug in Harrington's urine, it's looking like McNeil needs to come up with an alibi or a plausible explanation as to why it isn't him. McNeil claims he sourced the drugs on behalf of Petrov's guard, but he could be lying. And what about the guard who intercepted the food Rodriguez was taking to Petrov? Do we know who he is?'

'Go and find Middleton and see what Alex Petrov is planning. I'm not ready to put all my eggs in one basket,' she said.

Moretti nodded and prepared to leave.

CHAPTER TWENTY-FOUR

Moretti waited in the recess of a bedroom doorway until Middleton exited the corridor linking the panic room to the first-floor landing of the house. He'd guessed that she'd be there and as luck would have it, he was right.

'Sergeant, I wasn't expecting a police escort? Is there anything I can help you with?' Middleton said, brushing her hands down her skirt, startled at discovering Moretti lurking on the landing.

Moretti matched Middleton's stride as she exited the corridor and they entered the main landing.

'Solve the investigation? That would be helpful,' he said.

Middleton raised her eyebrows. 'Oh dear. No further forward, Detective?'

Moretti pursed his lips. 'Progress is being made. How was the elusive Mr Petrov?'

Middleton motioned with a sweep of her hand towards the smoking room and Moretti dutifully followed. He didn't know if Middleton was stalling or whether she was being protective of their privacy. Although the house was a sprawling maze of uninhabited rooms, it didn't feel private. She led him into the main smoking area and waited until the secret door closed behind them.

'All a bit smoke and dagger?' Moretti said, sitting down in what had become his seat of choice. It had a view of the only entrance and exit, and he could also see Middleton.

'Very droll, Detective. I've always worked under the premise that walls have ears, and this house has many walls. Thankfully the smoking room isn't frequented as much as it used to be. Wealthy and healthy being the reason our patrons stay away,' she said. Middleton sat crossing her leg over her thigh and adjusting her position, so Moretti was side on to her.

'Tell me more about your relationship with McNeil,' Moretti said.

'Straight to the point. Why?' Middleton said.

Moretti smiled. 'Because I'm investigating the murder of a woman on these premises and your lover is a suspect in our custody,' Moretti said, the smile fading from his face.

Middleton lit a cigarette and waved the smoke away from Moretti as she exhaled. She'd dispensed with any of her previous hostess courtesy, and Moretti hadn't brought his pipe and tobacco.

'My love life has no bearing on the murder of Charlotte Harrington. If, and I believe it's a big *if*, John killed her, then he deserves to rot in a prison cell and never see the light of day again. If I may be so bold, I think you've acted in haste, Nick. I don't believe for one minute John killed her and I think you feel the same. Must be tough on a man with intellect to be led and not lead,' she said.

Moretti refrained from comment. It was Middleton's way of baiting him and he knew it. Middleton knew nothing of the way he and Nash operated, and he intended to keep things that way. He didn't want this to be another casual chat. There'd be little bonhomie on this occasion. He was as keen as Nash, and the hierarchy of New Scotland Yard, to see the inquiry closed with the right suspect charged. He'd be civil. He always was, but he wanted Middleton to know that trust worked both ways. Moretti saw her actions of ferrying "supplies" to Petrov as an act of provocation. As far as Moretti was concerned, Petrov and son could slum it out in the panic room. The sooner they experienced a level of discomfort the better. A degree of hunger might cause them to venture out and see the realities of the situation they were in – living within the boundaries of a crime scene that occurred on their watch.

'Why didn't you question John about the bottle you saw in his cabin?' Moretti said.

Middleton shrugged. 'I told you. I had no reason to suspect it was anything other than a vessel out of its place. I'm not a seer, Sergeant. Had I known about the substance it contained, and for what purpose it could be used, I would have taken the appropriate action.'

Moretti leaned forwards in his seat, hands spread at his knees as though he was carrying an imaginary tray. 'What would that appropriate action have been?'

Middleton flicked ash into the ashtray and remained as she'd been sitting since their arrival.

'Not a clue. I've never been this close to a scene of crime let alone been under suspicion of involvement in it.' She raised her eyebrows and waited for Moretti to respond.

Moretti sat back and released a lengthy exhale. She was as cool as the tobacco humidifiers, her countenance unruffled.

He decided to change his line of questioning and steer it towards Petrov. 'What supplies were you taking to the panic room?'

Middleton blinked. 'A cake with a file secreted in it,' she quipped.

Moretti ignored her barbed reply. 'I'm waiting,' he said.

Middleton placed her cigarette in the ashtray and sat back. 'Alex Petrov wanted a list of all staff. He wished to check them against the original research document we returned prior to his arrival here. He also wanted more coffee and a change of towels,' she said.

'Where are the towels from the room? When I saw you earlier, I didn't see you with any,' Moretti said.

Middleton gave a short snort that caught Moretti off guard as her demeanour was usually controlled, self-assured.

'I sent them to the laundry chute. After all, if a client saw fit to utilise the safe room, as Mr Petrov has, they're entitled to clean linen no matter what crisis caused him to be in the room in the first place,' she said, as though speaking to a child.

Moretti laughed.

'So, you're telling me that any Heath Hall client, under imminent threat, has an expectation that their smalls will be cleaned, and new towels provided on request? How the other half live!' he said, shaking his head.

'Hospitality is clearly not an industry I recommend as alternative employment upon your retirement. Your manner is abrupt and obtuse. Mr Petrov is innocent until proven guilty. Isn't that right?' she said, her face as set as the stone pillars that adorned the pool area.

Moretti interlocked his fingers, elbows at rest on the arms of the leather tub chair.

'Look where being hospitable got Charlotte Harrington – murdered. I've a job to do and I won't rest until her killer is found. If that means shaking the very foundations of this luxury mausoleum, then so be it. I expected a level of cooperation when you led me in here. Now I see it was an act. An act you play with everyone who enters this house.'

Middleton stood and straightened her skirt. 'Unless you intend to arrest me, Sergeant, I'm free to leave. I agreed to remain within the walls of this house as an act of goodwill. An act I'm happy to rescind if you continue with this hostility. I appreciate the frustrations with your job, I experience similar difficulties daily, but I always remain professional. A trait you may wish to consider,' she said.

Moretti remained seated. Middleton didn't appear as though she was in any haste to leave the room. She picked up her cigarette holder from the ashtray and took a determined drag before raising her chin and blowing out the smoke towards an extractor in the ceiling.

'You're free to leave, yet you are the one choosing to remain. You intimate I'm in servitude to my bosses and the police as a whole and you couldn't be farther from the truth. I choose to be in the role I'm in and proud of it. I like seeing justice done for the public good. You on the other hand appear to enjoy nothing. I don't believe for one minute you get any sense of satisfaction out of pandering to every guest's whim and need. Yet here you are making sure Petrov's pillows are plump and his towels are fresh. I know which side of the fence I'd rather be on,' Moretti said.

Middleton's head snapped in Moretti's direction. He pushed himself out of his chair and stood. His instincts told him Middleton was about to strike. He'd triggered her wrath and was at risk of being on the physical end of it as a result, detective or otherwise. Middleton stepped within striking distance of Moretti, her shoulders firm as a vein pulsed visibly in her neck. Her breathing was rapid, and Moretti prepared himself, mentally, for an assault. Middleton momentarily turned her back before facing him again. She was composed and assured.

'Don't assume you know anything about me or my life from the brief time we've spent here. Don't confuse the catering of clients' needs with servitude to the rich either. I know my job and do it well. A key part of being a leader is to demonstrate that you are not above any task when the need requires it. I'm at skeleton staffing thanks to *your* security measures. No one in or out. That means those remaining have extra duties to perform. *You*, however, don't appear to have the ability to successfully investigate a piss-up in a brewery where there's only one person inebriated. Here you are stalking me in a corridor, questioning me about what items I'm taking to a guest and how they're being accommodated. Doesn't fill me with any hope that you're closer to discovering who killed Charlotte Harrington – a woman in a house with limited staff. It's no wonder there's no faith in policing in this country anymore,' she said.

Moretti stood and waited for Middleton to lead the way out. 'You have no idea what dealing with death entails. You cannot compare your role with mine.' A sense of unease broiled in his gut. This wasn't how he'd intended the conversation to go. He'd made an assumption about Middleton's character and that was something that didn't sit well with him. He investigated with an open mind but on this occasion he'd closed his mind down. Shutting off a world he had little direct experience of, deferring to societal prejudice on how the other half lived and how those who operated around the wealthy performed.

'Look, I didn't wish to cause offence,' he said.

Middleton stopped, turned, and smiled. 'I serve the living, you serve the dead. Both deserve the same degree of professionalism. On that we can agree,' she said, stepping aside to offer Moretti the exit first.

CHAPTER TWENTY-FIVE

Moretti opened his laptop, became frustrated with the time it was taking to power up, and promptly closed it. The sensation in his gut, after meeting Middleton, had shifted from unease to a burning feeling. The kind he had when a suspect walked free from court. It was rare, but nevertheless the sense of injustice ate away at him every time. He looked across at Nash who was smashing away at the keyboard of her own laptop. Moretti winced with every key she hammered.

'Jesus, Pip, any more force and you'll be through the table.'

Nash ignored him and continued with her frenzied jabbing. He left her to it. He hadn't the energy to engage with her and sat back in his seat, resting his head on the back of the chair. He stared at the ceiling as he rocked side to side while considering his next move.

His concentration was broken by the slam of Nash's palm on the table. 'What next, Nick?'

Moretti sat up. 'Are you a mind reader? I was struggling with the same question and hoping you'd come up with the answer to that.'

Nash pinched the bridge of her nose, squeezing her eyes for a second before she stood and began patrolling the room. Moretti noted how she held herself in a similar way to Middleton, assured and confident.

'That rant against the keyboard created an email to Commander Allen. He has a meeting with the commissioner in an hour and needed an urgent update on the state of play here. One minute I'm ordered off the case, then before I've had time to zip my bag shut and grab a handful of disposable pens, I'm required to remain and provide him with a breakdown of the inquiry. It's beyond frustrating. Our hands are tied, Nick. I can't waltz in and arrest Petrov. He's entitled to stay where he is and say nothing, as is his entire close protection team, one of whom happens to be his son. They're also free to leave, and if I'm honest, I wonder what's keeping him here. Why hasn't he left?'

Moretti scratched his forehead. 'A reasonable question. He's got money, influence, and power and yet he's choosing to remain in that suite. Do you know if he's under any kill contract? Could the death of Harrington be some kind of extreme threat to his life?'

Nash stopped tapping her pen against her teeth and wagged the tip towards Moretti. 'That's not an unreasonable suggestion, Nick. I know we shouldn't work on assumptions, but there's no doubt Petrov appears more comfortable remaining where he is than returning to Russia. I'm aware he's had several assets seized because of the current conflict in Ukraine, but he hasn't had his travel restricted. It would appear he does have access to money. Significant amounts of money to rent this place,' Nash said.

'What do we know about Harrington's finances? The letting agent for her property said she paid each month by standing order. Never defaulted in the two years she's rented the property,' Moretti said.

'Task the intelligence unit to provide a full financial breakdown of her assets. In particular, how much Petrov has invested in her as an employee. Also, ask them to conduct further research into her lifestyle to see if there's any pattern in her day that seems out of the ordinary. Places she often frequented and people she had regular contact with, and when. You know the drill,' Nash said.

Moretti opened his laptop. He waited for the machine to run through the laborious security checks before typing and sending the request while Nash waited. They were both interrupted by a light tap on the door to the meeting room. The knock on wood was swiftly followed by the door opening. Middleton bustled in, her manner that of a person who had business to attend to and wouldn't be thwarted in her pursuit of that aim.

'You do know this is a restricted area?' Nash said.

Middleton had reached the meeting table where the detectives sat. She leaned on the edge of it and frowned. 'You've made that as clear as the Heath Hall crystal, however, I thought you'd wish to know that there's a person at the front gates. They're claiming to be here on behalf of a Commander Allen. The armed uniform officer let me know via the gate's intercom. I took the liberty of having the communication system diverted to another room so you wouldn't be disturbed. Shall I let them in, or is that duty beyond my *restricted* access?' Middleton said.

Nash walked over to a monitor that was in the room and switched it on. The screen came to life displaying the main gates. The DPG officer who'd replaced Petrov's henchman appeared to be dancing with a male in a grey suit upon an invisible line. Nash noted how the suited man wasn't carrying a briefcase. He stopped his waltz to produce a mobile phone from his suit jacket pocket. After tapping at the screen, he held it to his ear turning his back to the uniform officer. There was a brief interlude then the officer on the gate leaned into his personal radio attached to his lapel, spoke, and stepped aside. The suited male nodded as he strode towards the main entrance.

'It would appear that the visitor has breached the gates. I'll meet him at the main door,' Nash said, nodding at Moretti to join her. Not that Nash couldn't handle herself in a confrontation, physically or verbally, but on this occasion she wished to have Moretti there as a witness to any conversation. She was beginning to feel outnumbered by busybodies within the walls of the house. Whenever she felt overwhelmed, she would use all she had in her arsenal to protect herself.

Nash arrived in time to hear a firm double tap on the wooden doors to the house. Not the usual three thumps she associated with a detective.

Nash opened one of the double doors. 'ID,' she said.

The male at the door removed a slim-framed pair of glasses he was wearing. He began to clean each lens with a handkerchief he'd removed from his suit jacket's outer pocket, meticulously working the cloth over each lens. 'DI Nash, I presume. Commander Allen warned me about you. Having communicated with a Ms Middleton via the intercom, I don't believe you are her.' He replaced his glasses and retrieved a sealed, plain white envelope from his inner pocket. He handed it to Nash.

'I thought there was a postal strike?' Nash said, refusing the envelope.

Moretti coughed into the crease of his elbow stifling the urge to laugh. This was a side to Nash he hadn't witnessed in a while.

The male flapped the envelope in Nash's direction as though he was drying a Polaroid picture.

'The time for flippancy is over, Inspector. This is a letter from the Home Office. It's been endorsed by Commander Allen. It gives me access to Mr Petrov with immediate effect. I suggest you take it and read it.'

Nash inhaled and took the letter. She opened it and extracted a headed sheet of paper embossed with the Home Office watermark. It was exactly as the man had stated. Mr Alexander Carter was granted access to Mr Petrov. Failure to assist Mr Carter would be seen as an obstruction of an official of His Majesty's Government and dealt with accordingly. What this meant, Nash didn't understand, but equally hadn't the will to test.

'I will need to make a phone call. I insist on you confirming you are the Mr Carter the letter refers to,' she said.

Carter nodded and produced a photo ID, again with the Home Office logo embossed into it. Nash handed the card to Moretti who left to make a call to confirm the legitimacy of the owner. Nash remained within the doorway. Neither she nor Carter spoke.

Moretti returned quickly. 'It all checks out, ma'am. Mr Carter belongs to the Foreign Office and Commander Allen's PA confirms the letter is genuine.'

Nash stepped aside and ushered Carter over the threshold and into what she regarded as her scene.

'Record Mr Carter in the scene log, Nick,' she said.

Nash showed Carter through to the room they were using.

'We have only been able to communicate with Mr Petrov via video-link,' she said. 'I will see if he's free and wishes to speak with you.'

'That won't be necessary. I have heard from his solicitor, and he is happy to talk with me in person. Please show me where he is.'

Nash paused over the screen's remote button. 'Mr Petrov has declined to speak with me or my sergeant since our arrival. He's invoking his right to diplomatic privilege. I don't see that changing for you.'

Carter smiled. 'I have more to offer Mr Petrov than you, Inspector.'

Nash observed Carter's stoic face. His expression left little to be interpreted from his flat demeanour.

'As you wish. My sergeant will show you to the suite. I remind you, Mr Carter, that I am investigating a murder. Regardless of your position within government, please don't make any promises that would compromise my investigation in any way.'

'I will act within the authority I have been granted by my position in government. Now, let me see Mr Petrov.'

Nash nodded at Moretti who swayed his hand indicating Carter should follow him.

* * *

Moretti led Carter out of the meeting room and up the central marble staircase, Moretti choosing to say nothing. He had formed an instant distrust of Carter and would wait to see how Petrov reacted after their meeting. So far, Petrov had stuck to his few words and kept contact with him and Nash to a minimum. Moretti wondered whether the reason Petrov remained in the panic room was because he was awaiting the arrival of a government official to guarantee him safe passage out of the UK and back to Russia. Moretti arrived at the door to the safe room and was surprised to find Middleton already there, arranging a hostess trolley laden with silver-lidded dishes and associated cutlery.

'Planning a party?' Moretti said, nodding at the array of dishes.

Middleton looked up from her trolley-organising. 'Very droll, Sergeant. I was asked by one of Mr Petrov's team to provide refreshments for a meeting. I see the guest has arrived,' she said, her focus shifting to Carter.

Moretti stepped aside as Middleton punched a key code into a numerical pad on the wall to the suite. Moretti watched as the door opened inwards and a dark-suited male came into view, arms loose by his side. Carter stepped forwards and the door closed after Middleton pushed the trolley in and remained with Moretti.

'I don't suppose there's any of that food left downstairs?' he asked.

Middleton raised her eyebrows. 'I thought the Met had their own mobile catering facilities? Perhaps it's time to call them in,' she said, walking away.

CHAPTER TWENTY-SIX

With the door to the safe room sealed, Carter raised his arms to allow the bodyguard to conduct an intensive pat-down of his upper body. Carter waited patiently as a wand used to detect metal was produced and waved over his body. Satisfied with his work, the bodyguard stepped aside and with a wave of his arm indicated that Carter was free to move within the confines of the suite. Carter strode along the suite's narrow corridor until he reached the living room where Petrov was standing, a cup of black coffee in hand, staring at a landscape painting that spanned most of the supporting wall.

Carter coughed into his sleeve. 'Mr Petrov, I trust you're well in the circumstances?'

Petrov remained with his back to Carter. He sipped his coffee and handed the cup to his son, Maxim, before turning to face his visitor.

'Mr Carter, we meet again. I am far from OK, as you well know.' Petrov's jaw twitched.

Carter shifted on his feet. Seeing an empty seat, he took the opportunity to make use of it. Petrov noted his guest's actions and maintained his position.

'It isn't the most ideal of situations you find yourself in, I grant you, but one that needs resolution,' Carter said, retrieving a plain sealed envelope from his jacket pocket. He handed it to Maxim who passed it to Petrov.

'What is this?' Petrov asked, tapping the envelope in the palm of his hand. 'A set of tickets to Verdi's *Rigoletto*?'

Carter raised his eyebrows. 'If only. It's a request for cooperation.'

Petrov squinted and stopped playing with the envelope. 'What type of cooperation?' he asked.

Carter sat back in the comfy chair he'd occupied and made a point of taking in the room for the first time. His arrival had been hurried and he'd had no time, or inclination, to assess his environment. He leaned forward to the edge of the seat. 'Your presence here is causing diplomatic rifts. Your legal rights remain unchanged. Your government are satisfied you need them and our government, well, let's just say they're figuring out what's best for them,' Carter said.

Petrov handed the letter back to Carter. 'I do not need anything from you or your government. They need me and my money more than I need them. You have nothing to give me that I don't already possess.'

Carter removed his glasses. He whipped the handkerchief from the suit pocket like a magician and began cleaning each lens, his concentration on this and not Petrov. Petrov let the silence hang long enough to feel he'd made the significance of his comment clear.

'You're wrong there, Mr Petrov. You're currently a suspect in a murder investigation. An investigation this government is keen to see resolved swiftly and justice done. You do understand where I'm coming from?'

Petrov stepped towards Carter. His path was blocked by Maxim who gently placed a hand on his father's chest, staring into his eyes pleading for calm. Petrov leaned against his son's hand before stepping to the side, away from Carter.

'I think you have said enough. I am not for threatening by any government. Please leave.'

Carter replaced his glasses, pocketed the handkerchief, and stood. 'If I were you, I would read the letter. If you admit to the murder, the government will do all it can to assist you. Read into that what you will. In any event the chances of you seeing a prison cell are remote. What our government won't tolerate is any increase of hostility between our two great nations, not over the death of anyone.'

Carter nodded and walked towards the corridor, leaving Petrov with his son. As he hit the centre of the corridor, he paused and turned. 'You have twenty-four hours to do the right thing, Mr Petrov, before both our governments become exasperated and take matters into their own hands. If that occurs, then all bets are off,' Carter said, then he turned and walked towards the exit to the suite.

Petrov waited until the suite door opened and closed. He held his breath expecting a show of force to remove him and when he realised this wasn't happening, he released a long and slow exhale. He took the letter and walked out of the living area into the main bedroom. He lay on the bed where he held the envelope to the overhead light.

The paper was too thick to see inside. He opened the envelope and removed a single sheet of plain paper. Upon it, written in ink, was a sentence, "Leave now." Signed by Carter. He breathed deeply and let the letter drop to the floor. He closed his eyes and remembered the last time he'd met Carter. Carter had dressed differently then. Smart, but fitting for the occasion. Petrov had been attending the opera in Covent Garden and was surprised to find Carter in the box he'd hired. Carter had been most persuasive and Petrov, in his desire to relax and listen to his favourite opera, had agreed he could remain. That was two decades ago. A time when he wasn't as prominent in society as he was now but was a rising star, something Carter and those within the security services knew made him an ideal recruit to their cause. Petrov also knew he wouldn't see Carter again. Petrov ripped the words from the page. A small enough square he was happy to chew and swallow without risk of it causing him harm.

CHAPTER TWENTY-SEVEN

Moretti watched as Carter exited the double gates at the end of the drive. There was a briskness to his pace; his demeanour that of a man in a hurry to get away from potential harm. He dipped his head and weaved through the remaining press officials that were outside. Heath Hall was gaining media attention, but both Moretti and Nash were aware it wasn't as prominent as they'd expect an incident like this to get. It wasn't an everyday case and when it involved public figures, they'd expected greater heat. Maybe the press office was doing a decent job of keeping the wolves from the door, for now at any rate. Whether this would alter after Carter's visit was anyone's guess.

Moretti observed the monitor. Carter turned right along The Bishops Avenue and was lost to his view. Moretti wondered why his meeting with Petrov had been so brief. Why would a government official go out of their way for such a short duration? They could have phoned; Petrov had the ability to communicate with whomever he wished while he was in the suite. Nash was limited in her legal powers to keep Petrov incommunicado. This wasn't a typical scenario involving a potential suspect for murder. In fact, none of this was proving to be typical at all. Both detectives were hampered by red tape and bureaucracy.

'What now, Pip?' Moretti said.

Nash stopped writing in her decision log and put her pen on the table. She removed a pair of reading glasses and pinched her tired eyes. 'I'm going to see Commander Allen. We can't operate under these constraints, Nick. While I'm away, get hold of Sagona in the incident room. Get him to put a search team on standby. Whatever the outcome of my meeting, I'm going back to Harrington's flat and ripping it apart. We've done all we can here, forensically. The arrival of this Mr Carter bothers me. I feel we're running out of time to get Charlotte Harrington the justice she deserves.'

'But we've been through her flat and there was nothing there,' Moretti said, with a note of exasperation.

Nash slid a printout across to Moretti who began to read the document.

'That's the initial financial analysis for Harrington. It's not what I expected. There's a distinct lack of transactions, in my opinion, which must mean she's either very astute with money or she has access to cash outside of this account – her only account by what we've established so far. She has one credit card to her name that's never been activated. You heard Middleton comment about Harrington's clothes, handmade she said. It doesn't sit right with me, Nick. Too many people at a very high level have an interest in this murder. I need to know why, and I won't stop until I have the answers,' she said.

Moretti put the sheet down on the desk and slid it back to Nash, 'We won't stop until we have the answers. There's no *I* in team, Pip,' he said.

Nash smiled back at him. 'On that note, Nick, I think you should know this could be my last case with you. If things go the way I expect with Allen, he'll have me off the homicide command the moment this is done. I'd rather make the choice to go myself than be pushed.'

Moretti leaned back in the chair and cradled his head in his hands as he rocked on the heels of his outstretched brogues. 'The job's fucked, Pip,' he said.

'It really is,' she said before adding, 'any thoughts on your own career path? Take this as an appraisal interview.' She smiled.

Moretti craned his neck and stared at the ornate ceiling. A chandelier of fine crystal droplets stretched down above him.

'In a word, none. I enjoy working with you so hadn't any desire to stop. Yes, I get pissed off with many aspects of the job, but not the opportunity to work with you, Pip,' he said, resting his head back towards Nash.

She felt a flush of warmth across her cheeks that extended down her neck and into her chest. She too enjoyed Moretti's company and hadn't anticipated how she might react to not having him by her side at work. Not that she was attached to him in any way. She wasn't. She was a capable and professional operator who adapted to her environment very well. She'd worked with a few DSs, but Moretti had saved her life on more than one occasion and when that occurs an invisible bond is formed.

There was a gentle tap at the door and both detectives turned to see Middleton's head appear around the edge of the now open door.

'Forgive the intrusion, but I thought you'd wish to know Mr Petrov is making preparations to return home,' she said as though addressing a staff team prior to cleaning the imminently vacant room.

No sooner had she finished, Nash's phone beeped. She glanced at her screen and saw a message from McNeil's custody officer.

Reminder that your detention time for McNeil is running out.

Nash placed her phone on the table. 'Let's get to work,' she said.

CHAPTER TWENTY-EIGHT

Moretti waited outside Harrington's flat along with four detectives Sagona had rallied together. They donned their forensic barrier clothing, checking each other to ensure there were no obvious rips or tears in the flimsy all-in-one suits. Satisfied they were ready, the scene guard stepped aside, Moretti unlocked the door to Harrington's apartment, and they entered. All was as they'd left it. As Moretti handed the scene log to the officer stationed on the door, he reflected on the job that lay ahead. It was never easy respecting the domain of the dead when gathering evidence, especially when the evidence they sought could be hidden. Nash had been unequivocal before she'd sent Moretti – leave no stone unturned. To him the message was clear. Rip the place apart and find the evidence.

Nash had cancelled her plans to doorstep Allen preferring to remain at Heath Hall while Petrov planned to leave. Moretti was quietly pleased that Petrov had started to make plans for his exit. It meant Nash would stay where she was and not wind Allen up further. Although Moretti celebrated variety in his private life, he relished stability at work. As he watched his team move into the kitchen to begin their search, he sensed a pride that they'd all volunteered to leave their tasks to join him. They were as passionate as he was to see justice done. Thankfully, Harrington's flat wasn't a sprawling mansion but a modest two-bed, spartanly furnished. But the search went on for several hours with little being found that would assist the investigation.

Moretti and DC Jones sat on the edge of Harrington's bed. The remaining detectives stayed in the living room, chatting. Every room in the flat had been searched to no avail. Each room was as clean as a laundered bedsheet. Moretti walked out of the flat, dropped the hood to his suit and ruffled his hair. It felt sticky from sweat. His team had done all they could. Before he called Nash with the news, he remembered McNeil. In particular how Petrov had been insistent on having Heath Hall searched by a dog before he arrived. He recalled how the area the ketamine was discovered in was only evident to a dog's nose. Moretti looked back into the hall of the flat and the tired detectives that now began to gather themselves to leave.

'Let's try one last thing before we call it quits,' he said to the group, all of whom nodded if somewhat despondently.

The search dog handler Moretti organised was more than happy to run his spaniel, Fergus, through the flat. If there was anything worth finding, Fergus would discover it, the handler confidently explained to Moretti. The squad huddled outside the main door to the flat as Fergus sat obediently at the feet of his handler staring up in anticipation of his release. Moretti was at pains to point out this was a victim's flat, but the hope was that if any money was hidden, the dog would find it.

Pitiful whimpers accompanied Fergus's keen disposition. Moretti was glad the jet-black cocker spaniel was small as there wasn't a vast area for the dog to work. With a wave of his hand, the handler sent Fergus to work.

Fergus motored off, tail windmilling as he scented his way along the hall. His handler followed while Moretti and his team waited, leaving dog and handler to do what they did best. A short time elapsed before Moretti heard the buoyant tones of the handler praising his dog.

'You can come in,' the handler said.

Moretti nodded to the detectives, and they entered the flat. They found the handler and an excited Fergus in the spare bedroom that Harrington had been using as an office. Fergus's nose was planted at the base of the skirting board behind the standing desk, his butt in the air, tail flailing against the legs.

'I haven't seen him this excited in weeks,' the handler said, nodding at his charge.

Moretti leaned over the desk and stared at where the dog was indicating.

'It's skirting board. Is there a scent on the wood?' Moretti asked, somewhat dejected.

The handler laughed. 'My bet is that the skirting comes away. Whatever Fergus has discovered is behind it,' he said, smiling with pride and anticipation of the big reveal.

Moretti stepped back and chinned the air at DC Jones. 'Let's see if he's right, shall we?' he said.

Jonesy moved the desk to the side and the handler grabbed Fergus by the collar dragging him gently away from the base of the cavity wall between the two bedrooms. Jonesy knelt at the skirting and ran his hands along the top. There was no dust. He discovered a small nick in the wood that looked as though a knife had been used in it to pry it away. It wasn't obvious unless you were at his level. Moretti had a DC retrieve a standard cutlery knife from the kitchen and handed it to Jonesy.

With minimal effort, a section of skirting lifted from the wall. Moretti could see that the design of the wood was bevelled at the rear to ensure it could be refitted. In essence it was made for a reason. To conceal what appeared to be a cavity, a brick's height from the floor to the base of the wall. Jonesy shone his torch in the space and reached in. He moved his hand about until he retrieved a section of twine. Pulling on it caused a clear durable plastic bag to be revealed. Jonesy dragged the bag clear of the wall and placed it on the desk. The officers gathered round to see what they'd found.

Within the bag were bundles of fifty-pound notes in five half-brick sizes, two mobile phones, a couple of passports and a handheld device that appeared to be smaller than the scanner Middleton had presented at Heath Hall.

Moretti turned to the handler. 'Are you happy this is it?'

The handler nodded. 'He's found what was here,' he said.

Moretti stepped outside the room and called Nash.

'Pip, we've got a problem,' he said.

CHAPTER TWENTY-NINE

Moretti dispatched the search team back to base with the exhibits from Harrington's flat, instructing DC Jones as to how he wanted forensics to look at the contents of the bag. The cash would need tracing and the mobile phones would need to be analysed along with the passports. Neither enquiry would be quick despite the nature of the crime. Murder in London was on the rise, with limited resources stretched beyond capacity. Yvonne, their SOCO, had said she'd try and pull strings to have the work expedited, but Moretti wasn't holding his breath.

He arrived back at Heath Hall to find Petrov was still in residence. Nash was busy in the meeting room going over the financial work supplied by Sagona. Moretti dropped his jacket on the back of a chair and removed his tie. Nash waited for him to sit before she spoke.

'A result then,' she said.

Moretti rubbed his chin. 'One way of looking at it, Pip. Yes, we've found the cash you suspect she was living off, but don't know where it came from, or why she had two phones hidden in a false wall, two passports and a scanner for listening devices,' he said.

Nash breathed deeply and exhaled slowly. 'I think our Ms Harrington was an asset, Nick. A source. Explains the volume of cash, phones, and nomadic lifestyle. Not a street source; a government source. Question is, which government,' she said, ruffling her hair.

'This is a nightmare, Nick. It's no wonder Allen is keen to see a resolution. Meanwhile we must mop up this mess with a bucket that's overflowing. The custody inspector is breathing down my neck about McNeil's detention time and, if I'm honest, we're struggling to hold him,' she said.

Moretti shrugged. 'We've still got a job to do, Pip. Charlotte Harrington was murdered. We don't know where, but from Dr King's report, she wasn't moved far from the pool given the lividity on her body. Even if she was a source, which we don't know, she didn't deserve to die at anyone's hands. We're running out of time. Once Petrov leaves, we're stuffed. No getting him back if we can prove it was him and even if we do while he's here, we can't charge him. So, what do we do?'

Nash stood up and pinched the bridge of her nose as she walked and thought. Moretti remained silent. He knew her well enough to give her space while she reflected. She paused at Moretti's side placing a hand on his shoulder.

'Hold the fort, Nick. Now you're back and Harrington's flat has been searched properly, I'm going to see Allen. Either we're free to investigate this death or we get removed from the investigation. I won't lose this fight, Nick. Trust me,' she said as she grabbed her bag and left Moretti to mind Petrov.

* * *

Nash wasted no time on arranging lifts, preferring to take the Northern line to Embankment where she'd have the space to formulate a plan of attack once she confronted Allen. The carriages were surprisingly empty, and she was glad of a seat. The sway of the train lulled her. She leaned into the seat. Her back and neck came to rest against the padding and the tension she'd been experiencing in her body relaxed. She recognised the toll policing was having on her energy levels, both mentally and physically. It was one thing investigating one murder after another, but having the additional stresses of dealing with outside influences in the guise of Allen was dragging her down.

She emerged from the underground at Embankment. Commuters were darting one way and another in an effort to avoid collision. Heads down, focussing on their phones. She escaped the main throngs that were exiting the station, crossing Embankment towards New Scotland Yard. The road traffic was heading towards Westminster Bridge, replacing the heavy foot traffic of the station. A moderate breeze ruffled her hair as she leaned in and walked, hands stuffed in the pockets of her coat, bag over her shoulder. The Thames was at high tide. The smell of the water rich and heady.

Every few feet, she glanced up to check her path. As she did, she noted a man, sat at a bench, looking out across the water. It wasn't unusual to see people on the benches occupying that stretch along the route, but this person had caught her attention. He was leaning forward, working a cloth over the lenses of a pair of glasses. Nash slowed her pace; she crossed the road to the footway opposite New Scotland Yard. She remained in a position to see the man's shoulders and the back of his torso. She put her reaction down to a gut feeling. Her anti-surveillance training for her role as an undercover officer had stressed the point of noting when a person was seen more than once in the same, or different location. This was no coincidence. She'd seen the person before.

Carter.

A mobile coffee wagon provided a good vantage point from which she could stop and observe him. She walked to the wagon and placed an order. Carter could be, innocently, sitting having a break, but Nash sensed otherwise. He placed his glasses back on. He was looking at the river and glancing in the direction of New Scotland Yard, so Nash deduced that he was waiting to meet someone. Her curiosity got the better of her and Nash decided to see if her instincts were correct and, more importantly, whom Carter was meeting. The barista handed her the Americano she had ordered and Nash sat at a metal table, continuing her observation of Carter. She was satisfied Carter hadn't followed her from Heath Hall. She was always careful when on public transport, staying aware of the possibility that she was being followed.

She didn't have to wait long before her intuition was confirmed. From the direction of New Scotland Yard, she noted the unmistakable stride of Commander Allen. Allen was no detective. His demeanour smacked of a man meeting a mistress for the first time in public. His head darted from right to left as he made his way, with purpose, in the direction of Carter. Nash switched her attention back to Carter and noted how Carter turned his head away from Allen the moment he clocked him. Her suspicions were confirmed when Allen plonked himself down next to Carter, head forwards, staring out of over the Thames.

Nash didn't need to hear what was being said. The meeting confirmed the collusion between her boss and Carter went beyond what she considered reasonable bounds. Why meet away from Allen's office? Why not see each other in Allen's office – a stone's throw from where they sat? It had started to drizzle. Hardly a great setting for a public meet.

Nash watched as the two men talked. Both avoided eye contact for much of the conversation. Every now and then they'd face each other, but the moment was fleeting. Nash could tell they were talking, despite her angle of view, as Allen had a habit of using his hands whenever he was emphasising a point.

Allen was the tenser of the two, sat straight whereas Carter leaned back, his arm draped across the bench. The meeting was swift, and Carter made a point of waiting for Allen to leave and get some distance between them before he stood. Nash watched as Allen left. She had come to see him, but now she'd witnessed this liaison she made the decision to leave Allen well alone. He was clearly riled. Any unannounced meeting was likely to end in disaster, for her.

She decided to use the opportunity to see where Carter went next. Part curiosity, and part hope that he'd confirm he was from the Foreign Office. The headquarters were situated in King Charles Street, so not far to walk. Nash grabbed her coffee from the table and prepared to conduct a loose foot-follow. She maintained a healthy distance from Carter and was surprised when he walked towards Parliament, turning left onto Westminster Bridge.

His pace was sedate and relaxed. Nash had to drop back regularly to ensure she didn't spook him. Once they were near St Thomas' Hospital, he headed towards Albert Embankment. Carter began stopping at windows to shops where he'd pause before continuing along the same route. Nash dropped back further, choosing to blend in behind a group of tourists. She watched as Carter entered a newsagent's and left quickly before resuming his course towards Vauxhall. This way of operating continued as he progressed. He was soon outside Tintagel House. Nash remembered this building from when it was owned by the police but it had now been taken over by a private company offering office space. Carter walked past the building. Nash left the tourists and crossed the road, choosing to give Carter as much room as possible. She also sensed which building he was headed to, and her stomach tingled as she formed the connection.

She watched as Carter approached the gate to the monumental art deco building that sat on the corner of Albert Embankment. She smiled savouring the warm glow that comes with the confirmation of her detective instinct as Carter moved to his right. He passed a security guard at a set of gates and entered the sanctuary of the Secret Intelligence Service headquarters.

CHAPTER THIRTY

Moretti stood in the garden near McNeil's cabin. He tapped the dregs of tobacco from his pipe against the heel of his hand. The charred leaves dropped close to the bushes. He refilled and lit up. He'd come outside to get some headspace. Petrov hadn't emerged from the safe room as expected. There was little point in remaining in the house to wave Petrov goodbye when he'd become part of the fixtures and fittings. It was warm, a late evening sun adding to the backdrop of tranquillity Moretti was enjoying in this manicured outside space. London could have moments like this.

Nash had messaged him to say she was on her way back to Heath Hall with news. What that news was, he didn't care to know until she arrived. After she'd revealed her days on the unit were numbered, Moretti didn't wish to hear anything of a negative nature from the bowels of New Scotland Yard.

Moretti had also made use of Nash's absence to evaluate his own career path. He was minded for a complete change too. Tired of murder and the politics of investigating it, he was keen to leave the city and start afresh. Somewhere new, rural even, with a different force. He had the background and skills that would be sought after by any county unit. Even if Nash changed her mind, he was getting close to moving on. He could move his boat without a problem and moor up wherever he'd be accepted.

His contemplation was interrupted by the crunch of pea-shingle, the sound of which Moretti had come to associate with the feline stalk of Lioness Middleton. Middleton rounded the beech hedge that acted as a windbreak for this section of the estate's grounds.

'Thought I'd find you here, I recognised the smoke signals,' she said. A hint of a smile flashed across her cheeks as she joined Moretti on the deck. She moved towards a swing chair where she dropped her shoes before curling her feet under her thighs relaxing herself into the cushioned back of the chair.

Moretti looked away while she adjusted the hem of her skirt. Middleton popped open a silver cigarette box, extracted a cigarette and leaned towards Moretti's lit Zippo. Her eyes met his as she inhaled. She sat backhanding the cigarette close to her shoulder, the smoke catching the temperate breeze, so it drifted away from them both.

'So, how's the inquiry going?' she said.

Moretti shrugged. 'It's making progress,' he said. He'd assessed Middleton's demure display as an act. A portrayal of an easy-going attitude to gain information. She was an attractive woman, a seasoned socialite. Moretti had concluded that Middleton would be effective at working any room and getting attention. She'd achieved the aim of gaining Moretti's, but she wouldn't get any more information about the investigation and in particular, McNeil. Moretti sensed she was on a fishing trip, and he wasn't prepared to be her lure.

Moretti re-lit his pipe blowing smoke into the air as he sat back on the steps of the deck. A silence rest in the air like their smoke upon the breeze. He'd come to see Middleton in a different light, one that meant she cast a shadow wherever she trod. His tactic of temporary muteness worked as expected.

'Nick, you don't mind if I call you Nick, do you? When will John, Mr McNeil, be released?'

Moretti stared ahead as he contemplated his reply.

'I've no idea. Why don't you phone the custody officer at Islington Police Station and ask them?'

Middleton flinched. 'I'm not his wife, they wouldn't speak to me.'

Moretti turned and faced her. 'So, you considered it?'

'Yes.'

'Even though he's a suspect in a murder investigation. A murder of a woman you knew and respected.'

Middleton flicked ash onto the deck. She leaned forwards on the swing seat. 'I don't believe he murdered her, and if you did, he'd have been charged by now.'

'Why do you think he didn't do it?'

Moretti fixed his eyes upon Middleton's as he waited for her reply.

'Because he's weak, that's why.'

'In your vast experience, weak men aren't capable of murder?' Moretti said, his tone playful.

Middleton smirked. 'I enjoy books and podcasts on true crime. None of the perpetrators that I found interesting would have been regarded as being of a weak disposition. McNeil is employed here because I got him the job. He left his last one due to stress.'

Moretti remained silent. Middleton on a mission was like the press, he thought, manipulative and one-sided in her opinion. Nothing he could say would shift it. He decided to change tactic.

'What will you do if he's charged?' he said.

Middleton's eyes flared. 'I think we both know that's unlikely, don't we?'

Moretti leaned against the wooden strut that supported a pergola which spanned the width of the deck. 'You don't know what I think. I'm asking for your view, not mine. Strange choice of man to have an affair with, if you ask me. I'd have expected a person with your means to have trawled a wider pool,' Moretti said.

Middleton's forehead pinched. Dropping her cigarette to the floor, she slipped her shoes on before grounding the remnants of the cigarette into the wood. She rose and straightened her skirt.

A surge of heat flushed through Moretti's chest. His arm and leg muscles tightened. He rose off the deck steps. He didn't wish to be at a disadvantage should Middleton choose to strike. Her breathing had become forced, as though she was preparing to squat for one last rep after a heavy legs session.

Middleton's breathing began to calm, her chest relaxing in its heave and fall. 'I'm sorry. You triggered something in me, I don't know what,' she said.

Moretti waited. Middleton paced the deck before sitting on the top step Moretti had occupied. Moretti sensed she'd managed to regulate herself enough for him to feel safe to join her. He sat next to her; a space between them denoted personal boundaries were being respected.

'I'm no angel, Sergeant, and I'm not proud of my affair with John. He provides comfort. I've been hurt in the past. As a result, I find myself attracted to men whom society looks down upon,' she said.

Moretti stared ahead. 'How long have you and John been together?'

'Long enough to care.' She picked at her dress and fussed with her hands before releasing her tension and placing them loosely at her knees.

Moretti wasn't one for affairs, but he'd witnessed his fair share of them in the job.

'Does anyone know about you and McNeil?'

Middleton sighed. 'I'm very good at my job, Sergeant. Discretion is everything. That's been my mantra for life. If anyone did know, I'd be very surprised. John wasn't required for every guest. Mr Petrov was a guaranteed contract. I'd arrange any others on an ad-hoc basis or whenever I felt like company here. It's a lonely role and I have needs too.'

'Have you spoken to anyone about you and John?'

Middleton tilted her head slightly as she eyed Moretti. 'Who would I tell and why?'

Moretti remained impassive. 'Everyone I've met who's in a relationship, regardless of circumstances, has had someone they've confided in. It's a natural human need to feel validated.'

'I don't need external validation; however, I think Charlotte suspected something.'

Moretti let the statement hang before he replied. 'Go on,' he said, leaning against the deck post so he could see Middleton as she spoke.

'I was here, with John, the last time Mr Petrov was over. John had his hand atop of mine as Charlotte rounded the beech hedge. He withdrew it too quickly. I noted her face looked shocked. A woman knows these things, Sergeant, and she is, was, no fool. She flashed me a wry smile and that was all I needed in confirmation. She never brought the subject up and I neither. Two people aware that we had a job to do, and as long as we remained professional, we'd continue to get on well together. As I said before, I valued Charlotte. I enjoyed her company when she was here.'

'Did you talk about it with John?'

'No. He mentioned something along the lines of "close call", when we were alone that evening, but we had more pressing things to do, and little time left. Let's leave it at that,' she said, looking away from Moretti across at the gardens.

Moretti got up. He offered Middleton a hand, and she accepted it. He steadied her by the forearm as she rose from the step, then let go of her once she was standing.

'Have you spoken with Petrov since I last saw you with his fresh towels?' Moretti said.

'I spoke with him by phone before coming here. He was asking about your counterpart, Nash. He wishes to speak with her,' she said.

Moretti squinted. 'An earlier heads-up would have been appreciated,' he said, stuffing his spent pipe into his outside suit pocket.

'I was enjoying our conversation and your boss is away,' she said, leading the way back towards the main house.

Moretti walked alongside her tapping out a message to Nash on his phone while Middleton pointed out various flora and fauna as if they were on a horticultural field trip. They parted ways at the house with Middleton going to the kitchen while Moretti returned to their temporary incident room.

CHAPTER THIRTY-ONE

Nash sat at the head of the meeting table as Moretti updated her on his conversation with Middleton. Once he'd finished, she fed back her observations from her time in London.

Moretti raised his eyebrows. 'Sneaky,' he said, on hearing where Carter had returned to. 'So where does that leave us? We're treading in murky water, Pip, with no chance of seeing the silt.'

Nash nodded. 'Very poetic, Nick. Middleton has clearly made an impression on you.' She smirked. 'Let's see what Petrov wants, shall we?'

Nash strode over to the Petrov phone, as they'd labelled it, picked up the receiver and pressed zero. There was a short interval before it was answered by a gruff sounding male with a Russian accent.

'Yes?'

'It's DI Nash. I've been informed Mr Petrov wishes to speak with me?'

The male on the end of the line cleared his throat. 'This is correct. He will see you in the secure room. You come without your detective. You will be searched before entering. No mobile phones. Those are his terms, do you agree?'

Nash glanced at Moretti who couldn't hear the call. She needed to reinforce, in her mind, that he was a key element of her team before she made her decision. A decision she didn't want to take, but knew she had to if she stood any chance of breaking the stalemate in her inquiry.

Nash inhaled deeply. 'I agree. When?'

There was a pause before the male replied, 'Now would be a good time.'

'Very well,' Nash said, replacing the phone.

'Are we on?' Moretti asked, reaching for the suit jacket he'd draped over the back of an adjacent chair.

Nash grabbed her own jacket from a coat rail hanger, feeding her arms into each sleeve. Once it was on, she flicked her hair out of the collar and adjusted the fit.

'So, it's just you then?' Moretti said, dropping his jacket on the table.

'How did you guess?' Nash said.

Moretti leaned against the edge of the table; shoulders slumped.

'The silent treatment and the way you push your shoulders back like you're prepping for a solo fight.'

Nash swallowed. 'I know you're disappointed. It's a game, Nick, nothing more. Petrov thinks he's in charge. He's asked for me. I'm in charge of this investigation, and he wants more control. We're a team, but on this occasion, I need you here, monitoring Petrov remotely,' Nash said.

Moretti's sallow demeanour flickered back to life. He sat back in the chair and faced Nash.

'Go on,' he said.

Nash sat next to him and leaned in. 'Audio only. Middleton may barge in, and I don't want the screen on. I'll be fine. Petrov may be an arsehole, but he's no fool. Last thing he'll want is any further diplomatic incident beyond suspicion of murder, especially harming the detective in charge of the inquiry. My hunch is that he wants to bargain in some way. Granted, he has diplomatic immunity, but his visit from Carter has clearly unsettled him.'

Moretti remained silent as Nash paused her deliberations. They'd worked together long enough to know how each other operated. This learned behaviour meant they knew when it was appropriate to comment and when to shut up and listen.

'Listen and note. Don't record it electronically. If it concerns Carter, then the less that's recorded the better. I may not approve of Petrov, but I do value the system of covert human intelligence sources. Let's maintain that, while keeping an open mind as to our inquiry and Harrington's right to an effective investigation. Her killer is close, Nick. Having witnessed Carter and Allen together I'm certain there's a cover-up taking place. Whether it's a necessary and proportionate response in law or arse-covering, I don't know, but we will do all we can to establish the facts,' she said.

Nash handed Moretti her job phone and personal one. Moretti switched them off.

'I don't want to be interrupted while you're with Petrov. I need to focus. Having an ear open for your phone going off won't help,' Moretti said.

Nash nodded and left Moretti to establish the link with the room in a way Petrov wouldn't be aware of. Middleton had alluded to the one-way audio when she'd explained the system and Moretti had a good memory for details.

***

Nash stood patiently outside the suite picking at a stray hair on her jacket. A show of appearing nonchalant as she awaited the arrival of one of Petrov's goons to let her in. She didn't knock. They were expecting her. She knew the door was hooked up visually on the inside. After all, you wouldn't have a safe room without the facility to remotely see who was approaching. That would be foolish. She leaned against the wall and stretched her right calf muscle. She'd missed her daily run and longed to be away from the confines of Heath Hall and London. The politics of the police and especially Commander Allen had become a burden she wished to shed.

Her self-care was interrupted by the click of the door lock to the suite. She pushed away from the wall as the door opened. She recognised Petrov's son, who framed the entrance. He held a search wand in his right hand that he waved at Nash to summon her forwards. Nash was keen to comment that she was neither a dog seeking a game of fetch, nor a fly to be swatted. She refrained from voicing it though; it would be lost in interpretation and wouldn't change the circumstances in her favour. Instead, she stepped forwards and held her arms out to the side. Maxim waved the wand over her body as Nash stood and stared along the corridor towards the main room of the suite. A tension nipped at her stomach.

Maxim stood from a dip as he scanned her feet and nodded. 'You may continue. Mr Petrov is waiting for you in the living room.'

Nash didn't respond, choosing to ignore the bodyguard regardless of his family association with Petrov. She walked to the living room where she was met by another bodyguard who stood aside. She continued to where Alex Petrov was standing by a hostess trolley.

'Coffee, Inspector?'

Nash looked at the ornate silver set on the trolley. Her mind turned to the possibility she could be drugged or poisoned. She hesitated, then dismissed the fleeting angst of her overwrought mind.

'Thank you. No milk or sugar,' she said.

Petrov poured a cup and handed it to her.

'I made it myself, you have nothing to fear,' he said, as though he'd read her mind. 'Not all Russians are assassins or ruthless killers,' he continued, walking towards a pair of seats either side of a low oak coffee table.

He sat down and Nash did too. Both bodyguards left the room, closing the door to the suite.

'We are free to speak. My men will not disturb us.'

Nash placed her cup on the table and leaned back. 'It was you who wanted to talk, so the floor is yours, as we say in the UK.'

Petrov smiled, leaning back, and turning to the side where he crossed his leg over his thigh.

'You believe I killed Charlotte Harrington and that is why I'm staying here, protecting myself with the foolish laws of your country. Hiding behind immunity for foreign diplomats. You are misguided.' Petrov paused, took a drink of coffee, and set his cup back on the table.

Nash remained as she sat, observing Petrov's body language. If he was a poker player, he'd be a strong adversary. She decided to speak.

'What I believe, is known only to me. If you've decided to fish for information, then you've come to the wrong lake. You've made it clear where you stand in terms of my investigation. As far as I'm aware your political status hasn't changed, unless your last visitor told you otherwise?'

Petrov looked away, and Nash noted his Adam's apple dip and rise, signs she'd hit a nerve. Petrov rubbed his jaw. Nash waited for him to reply. She was in no rush. Allen was breathing down her neck and sooner or later the inquiry would come crashing down around her. The tension she'd experienced in her stomach while she'd waited outside the suite had abated now she was incarcerated in the room with the oligarch. There was something strangely comforting about being within the security of the suite, despite the company she kept.

Petrov stood and Nash remained seated. He walked towards a print of what appeared to Nash to be a bronze figure with arms held to the side, holding weighing scales. Within the scales was a set of eggs on one side, and on the other, hatchlings. Below the hatchlings were two men who appeared to be in conversation. Petrov pointed at the picture and turned to Nash.

'This print is by Vladimir Kush. Are you aware of his work?'

'Murder in London prevents me from visiting galleries. My earnings wouldn't warrant spending on fine art,' she said.

Petrov smiled.

'This is a print. I had it put here for when I visit. It is called *Pros and Cons*. The figure on the painting resembles the goddess of Justice. The two men are disputing the eternal question of life. One philosopher is pointing to the sky, preferring the heavenly beginning, and the other is pointing down, considering the earthly beginning. Whatever the debate, neither will agree.' He inhaled and let out a sigh.

Nash stood and joined him by the image. It was certainly impressive the closer she stood to it.

'Why did you want this print here?'

Petrov folded his arms. 'As a reminder. I knew a time would come when I too would have to make a life choice. I knew it would be here and not in Russia. I cannot explain how I knew, but I did. This picture also hangs in my own security bunker at home in Russia. If you'd lived my life, you would understand. This has nothing to do with the death of Charlotte Harrington. I have nothing to do with her death, but I do have choices to make, especially when it comes to my life and my security. On these issues, I'm sure you will appreciate where I'm coming from, Inspector Nash.'

Nash watched as Petrov walked back to his seat and dropped into the chair. She wasn't sure she did understand what Petrov was intimating but could only surmise his meeting with Carter hadn't gone as he wished. Was the UK government seeking to give up his immunity? If she asked this, Petrov would know she'd done some digging into Carter's background. Petrov was no fool. He'd expect Nash to do some basic checks before allowing Carter into Heath Hall to meet face to face with him. Petrov wasn't to know that Nash had worked out who Carter was and that he was certainly in a covert relationship with Petrov. Whether in the stages of initial recruitment or something longstanding, she hadn't established and was unlikely to. What she could be certain of was that the cards she held would remain close to her chest at this stage.

'You told me you entered this suite to protect yourself from harm. I informed you that your security was taken care of. Protection above and beyond what most citizens have in the UK. There are specialist armed police officers on the estate linked to the largest security organisation in London, yet you remain here despite your diplomatic status and obvious resources to leave, why?'

Petrov leaned forwards and took the coffee cup in his hands. It was tepid and Nash sensed he hadn't the desire to get a fresh one.

'My safety is mine to control. I invited you here to tell you I didn't kill Charlotte Harrington. I'm telling you this, wishing to see justice done. Something I know you believe in too. Why else would you do your job? You have kept your word with me, Inspector, where others have not. I am simply returning this hospitality by having this meeting and making this statement to you. I didn't have to speak with you and certainly didn't need to deny my involvement in the tragic death of Charlotte Harrington in this way. You understand? Look elsewhere, Inspector, that is my message to you. Your killer isn't in this room.'

With that, Petrov stood. Nash recognised this universal sign that their meeting was over. She stretched from her chair, glancing back at the picture and then at Petrov.

'Scales represent justice to me too. Those scales hold the balance between life and death and yet, not every egg hatches even when given the greatest of parental care. I've heard what you've had to say, Mr Petrov, and I appreciate your desire to see Charlotte's death investigated fully. I will remain open to who, or where, her killer is. I will ask one thing of you while I close this case,' she said.

Petrov held his hands open towards her. 'What is this one thing?'

'That you remain here until I establish who killed her and how.'

Petrov looked at the painting and back at Nash.

'I'm interested to see which way the scales tip, Inspector. I will honour this request for twenty-four hours only. Once this time is finished, I will leave and there's nothing you can do to prevent this from happening,' he said, nodding in a bow.

Nash returned the gesture. Petrov said something in Russian and the two bodyguards returned and escorted her out of the panic room.

CHAPTER THIRTY-TWO

Nash returned to the meeting room to find Moretti busy at his laptop reading updates from the inside team at Hendon. He turned as Nash entered and closed his computer down. 'So the clock is ticking?' he said.

Nash took off her jacket and draped it over the back of a chair.

'In terms of Petrov, yes. We always have been up against time, so it comes as no shock to me. I think he was telling me he's leaving and applying a timeframe around it, so I don't frustrate his exit. Not that I could,' Nash said.

'The Heath Hall staff are going to want to know when they can leave, Pip. We can't detain them any longer now we've spoken to them. They haven't asked to go, they're getting paid good money to be here, but that will end when Petrov leaves. Twenty-four hours isn't going to help us,' he said.

Nash walked across to the window that overlooked the gardens. 'We won't need twenty-four hours, Nick. Petrov was telling me something up there, he was wary, and I haven't worked out what it is he was trying to get across. I think we have the evidence, but it's more like staring at a jigsaw that's been scattered across the floor and we need to join the pieces up. Anything from the inside team? Any updates from Yvonne with our forensics?'

Moretti joined her at the window. 'The CCTV guys have come back. The systems are blank. They're doing their best to recover them, but it looks doubtful they'll succeed,' he said.

Nash rubbed her temples. 'What's the rest of the news?' she said.

Moretti raised his eyebrows. 'How did you know there was more?'

'It's in the tone of your voice, Nick. I can always tell when you're giving me news I don't want to hear.'

Moretti smiled. 'You're right, it gets worse. The dark hair from Harrington's neck isn't a match with Bliss, McNeil's spaniel. They're conducting further work. That's all they'd say,' he said.

'So that leaves us with what?' Nash said.

Moretti scratched the side of his neck. 'The ligature used is unknown, where Harrington was killed is the same. The bag taken from her flat needs examining as well as the folder from McNeil's house. In particular, whose hand Maxim was holding in the cropped picture.'

'Why that?' Nash said, turning to Moretti.

Moretti caught her gaze. 'Like you said, there are missing pieces of the puzzle preventing the full picture from being revealed. I tasked Sagona with chasing up the outstanding lines of inquiry before you returned. It's a matter of time before we get answers. Whether they're the answers we want, remains to be seen.'

Nash walked over to the table, opened her decision log, and wrote an update with what they'd discussed and her meeting with Petrov.

'Let's see if McNeil remembers who was in the photo and why he kept the folder at home. Get JJ and Jonesy back here while we speak to McNeil. Tell them to bring the folder found at McNeil's place too,' she said.

Moretti called the custody officer and informed her they'd be over to interview within the hour. He then tasked Sagona to get the detectives over to Heath Hall so they could leave.

* * *

McNeil appeared in sombre mood as Nash and Moretti began the preamble to the recorded interview. Nash decided she'd lead.

'Mr McNeil, we would like your help in relation to the contents of a folder found at your house, in particular a photo of one of Petrov's bodyguards,' she said, passing a copy of the cutting across the table to McNeil.

McNeil looked at it and pushed it back to Nash.

'What about it?'

'Why do you have it?'

'It's the first time I've seen it.'

'It was found in your house.'

'Like I said, it's not my folder. I don't know what's in it, and that's the first time I've seen the photo. I know where it was taken though.'

'Go on,' Nash said.

'It was outside a private club in London. I was asked to drive for Maxim, Petrov's son, the guy in the picture. There was a confrontation with a photographer as he left. The photographer agreed to crop the photo if he went to press.'

'Who did he leave with?' Nash said.

McNeil looked away then back at Nash. 'Charlotte Harrington,' he said.

Nash leaned back in her seat. 'So Petrov's son knew our victim on a personal level, and you chose to say nothing about that until now?' she said, incredulous.

'I'm the one sat here, in custody. You're the detectives. It's the first time you asked me, and I've answered. What's bothering me now is that you didn't know he had a son, and said son is at Heath Hall. Also, that you appear unconcerned about how that photo ended up in my house when I didn't put it there,' he said, tutting as he mirrored Nash in his own seat.

Nash leaned forwards and tapped the photo with her pen. 'What was Maxim's relationship to Charlotte?' she said.

McNeil shrugged. 'Not a relationship, as such, more a trusted companion to go clubbing with.'

'So why all the insistence that the image be cropped if he was just out enjoying himself?' Nash said.

McNeil's eyebrows joined as he thought.

'I wasn't the one who insisted on it. When we got back, Middleton asked me how things went, and I told her. She was the one who got the photo edited. Arranged a decent sum of money with the photographer from what I can gather. I took the money to him. He's a regular outside the club; he gets good scoops from celebrities leaving pissed with the wrong person in tow.'

'Charlotte is hardly the wrong person if Alex Petrov knows her?' Nash said.

'I do as I'm asked when I'm here. Don't question, do. I guess I took that too far when I arranged for the ketamine to be left where it was, something I truly regret. I thought it was for Maxim, you know, for when he was going out on the town, that sort of thing. Not murder. Look, I've been your side of the desk, I'm not a killer. I have been stupid on this occasion; I'll grant you that. I'm trying to help here, I really am. Last thing I want is to be charged with a crime I didn't commit. That's the truth, take it or leave it,' he said.

Nash looked at Moretti.

'One last question before we finish this interview. Why did you have a new lead when we arrested you?' Moretti said.

McNeil frowned. 'I'd have sworn it was in my van, but I must have put the new one in and not my old one. That's the only explanation I can give. When I left home, I was late. I must have grabbed the new one by mistake,' he said.

'Thanks,' Moretti said and terminated the interview.

CHAPTER THIRTY-THREE

Nash watched as the gaoler bolted the door to McNeil's cell. The unease in her gut had returned and she wondered if the pressure of such a high-profile case was getting to her. Nash left the custody area and found Moretti in the intelligence room. He put down the phone he'd called Sagona on and faced Nash.

'Sagona has been cracking his whip. Yvonne has the results of the leads taken from McNeil's van. There's a DNA match on a tracking lead for Harrington and traces of dark hair similar to the one found on her neck.' Moretti beamed.

Nash acknowledged she'd heard him.

'Well, don't appear too overjoyed whatever you do, Pip. McNeil's banged to rights. He's a liar and we have the evidence. It's obviously a lie about having a different lead on him. He had the new one so we wouldn't link him to her death. Finally, the pieces are coming together,' Moretti said, rubbing the palms of his hands together as though trying to start a fire.

Nash sat down and Moretti stopped his hand rubbing.

'What's wrong? I thought you'd be over the moon with the breakthrough?' he said.

Nash licked her lips. 'Don't get me wrong, it's great we have the ligature. Just because it was found in McNeil's van doesn't mean he used it. That's my issue, Nick. He was very convincing in that last interview. What if we have the wrong suspect?' she said.

Moretti rubbed his jaw. 'Wouldn't be the first time,' he said.

Nash shook her head. 'I'm serious, Nick. I admit, when you questioned my choice of timing, I did arrest in haste. Something's not sitting well with me, and I can't put my finger on it.'

'Pip, we have him sourcing ketamine and the ligature was in his van. The drug was found in Harrington's urine, and the ligature is forensically linked to him and her. Once Allen knows this, he'll insist we get the CPS to authorise charges. I don't have an issue with it.'

'What about him denying the blue folder and newspaper cuttings in his house were his? Is that not odd to you?'

'Smacks of deflection on his part. Send us down a new road knowing the time he can be legally held in custody is running out. He knows the system, Pip. He's lying. Maybe he kept the cuttings and photo as a memento of sorts, I don't know. How else would it get there and for what purpose?'

Nash couldn't answer. Her mind was unable to counter Moretti's reasonable explanation. And he was right. Once Allen caught a sniff of the forensic evidence, he'd do what Moretti said. She couldn't have that happen without being sure McNeil killed Harrington, why, and how. Motive was missing and Nash needed this as much as the evidence.

Nash stood and stretched. 'Let's use this time to examine what was found at Harrington's flat. We'll stop off at Hendon before we return to Heath Hall.'

Moretti jangled the car keys. 'Your driver is ready, ma'am,' he said.

CHAPTER THIRTY-FOUR

Moretti parked in the parade square and killed the engine to the car. Both detectives got out and Moretti stood admiring the familiar lights that illuminated the second floor of the building their team occupied. A sense of pride flushed his chest. Pride for a team that, despite his and Nash's absence, had been steadfast in their endeavours at the coalface while the two of them managed events at Heath Hall. Without them they couldn't operate effectively – even when it felt as though the investigation had stalled, there was a squad doing all they could to find the right key to unlock the inquiry again.

They entered the exhibits room and located the clear bag found at Harrington's flat. They double-gloved and Moretti opened their exhibits bag and then the bag the money and passports were in. Moretti brought out the passports and took them over to a clear table where Nash laid out a sheet of white paper. They sat, placing the passports flat on the white sheet as they leafed through the pages. Neither said anything to the other as they conducted the task. After a short time examining the exhibit, they turned and acknowledged each other. Moretti was the first to speak.

'You'll never guess whose passport I have here?' he said.

Nash smiled and turned the picture of the one she'd opened towards him. 'Snap?' she said, smiling.

They packaged up the exhibits and left them in the cage, both exhilarated at what they'd discovered. Nash called Sagona instructing him to call in the team for an urgent briefing. In the interim period, Nash spoke with Moretti agreeing a strategy from this point forward. Both detectives were confident that Petrov's twenty-four-hour deadline was about to be smashed out of the park. She messaged Jonesy and told him to gather all the staff together at Heath Hall in an hour and not before.

* * *

Nash waited until her team had settled down before she began the briefing. She'd dispatched Moretti to Heath Hall. She felt energised now she was back among her troops and out of the restricted and fake environs of Heath Hall. She'd considered calling her DCI and updating him, but decided *fuck him*. He could hear about it all in the morning briefing along with Commander Allen. It was eleven at night. This could wait. Notifying them wasn't her priority. She opened the briefing to inform her team about the operation that would take place that evening.

'I'll keep this as short as I can. As you are aware, we've been up against it with this inquiry from the outset. You've all been diligent in the tasks you've been sent while we were at Heath Hall. Trust me when I say I'd have rather been here.'

Rumblings of dissent ran around the room before Nash continued, 'As you are aware, we've had John McNeil, the private security man, in custody. He's admitted to supplying ketamine, but not murder. A lead found in his van has been forensically examined and traces of Harrington's DNA, as well as dark hairs matching the one on her neck have been found. The width measurements of the lead fit those Dr King recorded on Harrington's neck. The leather tannin is also a match for what was swabbed from her skin. McNeil will remain in custody until tonight's operation is complete.'

A sea of nodding heads indicated they all understood. The next thing she had to say was the message she wasn't looking forward to.

'As you are also aware, there's been a considerable amount of interest in the case from His Majesty's

Government as well as our own Commander Allen. Due to the politically sensitive nature of the investigation and potential economic damage to the UK, I have designated this part of the inquiry as confidential. To that aim, I am unable to include you in how it will progress from here. Until I have our suspect in custody, it will be run as a confidential operation. Once I have our suspect in custody you'll be briefed by George Sagona as to where I'll need you next,' she said.

Sagona was beaming that he'd hear the outcome before them, while the team groaned but understood. They'd had similar briefings in the past and it wasn't unusual practice for them. It also meant they could down tools until Sagona told them which ones they'd need. Calls home could be made, and families reassured they'd be home quicker than they'd initially expected. When that would be was still unknown. Nash looked at her watch and concluded the briefing. The team all parted ways and Nash exited the building and returned to her car where she called Moretti.

'We're good to go as of now. I'm on my way,' she said. As she exited the gates to the car park, she activated the blue lights. The front grille to the vehicle flashed blue, while the headlights alternated between dipped and full beam. The two-tone siren wailed as it pierced the evening air. She floored the accelerator and headed towards Heath Hall and what she hoped would be her finest hour.

CHAPTER THIRTY-FIVE

Moretti waited in a side road, ensconced in a nondescript vehicle that Jonesy and JJ had arrived in. He had the driver's window down and rested his elbow on the frame as he waited on a text message from Jonesy inside Heath

Hall. He'd already had one message informing him that all the Heath Hall staff were present in the meeting room waiting for him and Nash to arrive. Moretti's phone pinged with a message from Nash. She was ten minutes away from his location. He acknowledged her message and called Jonesy.

'I'm delivering the message now,' Moretti said.

'Understood,' Jonesy said, terminating the call.

Moretti dialled into the meeting room. Jonesy answered the phone then handed the receiver to Middleton.

'How can I help, Sergeant?' she said.

'All of you can leave Heath Hall. We'll be in touch should we need to speak further,' he said.

'I don't understand. Does Mr Petrov know?'

'Mr Petrov has his own lines of communication, as you are aware. I'm sure he knows his rights. He can choose to remain if he wishes, as can your staff, should they need to be of service to him. The choice is up to them,' Moretti said.

There was a pause on the line before Middleton replied, 'This all seems a bit abrupt. Have you charged someone?'

Moretti took a few breaths before replying, 'It's looking imminent that we do.'

'That can only mean one person then. Now I understand why you're telling me, Nick. Thank you,' she said.

Moretti asked for Jonesy, and he came back on the line.

'We're on. Message me when they leave,' he said.

'Will do,' Jonesy said.

The line went dead just as Nash, silently, drew alongside Moretti's car causing him to remove his elbow at speed from the open window frame. 'That was close,' he said.

'My arrival or shaving your elbow?' Nash said across her open passenger window as she reversed behind Moretti's car.

Moretti left his vehicle and got in Nash's car.

'I hope we're right about this,' Nash said.

Moretti raked the passenger seat back to full extension. His phone pinged and he opened the message. 'We're about to find out,' he said, pointing towards a concealed entrance within the wall that surrounded the gardens of the estate.

They were a sufficient distance away not to be observed from the gateway. A couple of press bods concentrated on the gate in front and nothing else. The detectives watched as the gate opened and their subject pushed past the reporters, head down, striding towards Kenwood House. Moretti got out of their car and followed on foot leaving Nash in their vehicle.

Their subject kept to the path that skirted the boundary of Kenwood House until they were a sufficient distance from Heath Hall. They looked around before ducking under the bough of some trees where they produced a phone. Moretti hung back. He couldn't hear what they were saying, but he could see from the subject's body language that the conversation was animated. Moretti sensed the person on the other end of the line was attempting to placate and calm the other.

Moretti called Nash. 'I think our target is going to meet someone. They're clearly agitated and looking around as though trying to identify a landmark as a reference point,' he said.

'OK. Don't lose sight of the target. I'm nearby,' Nash said.

Moretti killed the call. His thoughts proved to be correct. Within minutes a taxi pulled up and their subject got in the empty cab and the vehicle pulled away. Nash must have been close as she drew alongside Moretti. He got in the front passenger seat and Nash set off keeping the cab in view as it headed towards Hampstead. They followed the cab until it veered down a side road then drew up outside an opulent Georgian house in a quiet street. Security lights activated from the gated yard. Their subject got out of the cab and the vehicle departed.

'What now?' Moretti said.

'Let's see,' Nash said, pulling over a good distance away, but keeping the subject within view, and killing the headlights.

They didn't have to wait long before the person was approached by a lone male. The man hadn't been dropped off by car, at least not close to where Nash and Moretti were parked. They waited as the two people remained in the street. Overhead street lighting provided them with a reasonable view. The man who'd joined their subject was wearing a trilby hat pulled down at the front, glasses, and a trench coat. A short conversation took place before the trilby-hatted male handed over a parcel, turned, so that their face could be seen by Nash and Moretti, before leaving on foot in the direction they'd approached from.

Moretti turned to Nash. 'Jesus,' Moretti exclaimed.

'Not Jesus, Nick. Carter,' Nash said.

CHAPTER THIRTY-SIX

Nash and Moretti watched as their subject loitered for a while before leaving on foot in the opposite direction to Carter.

'This is deep shit, Pip. We should call this off now before it explodes in our faces,' Moretti said.

'Where's the maverick Moretti I know?' Nash said.

'There's maverick and there's bloody stupid, Pip. You said this would all play out and we could put the job to bed without any hassle. I'm beginning to doubt your enthusiasm,' Moretti said.

Nash turned side on in the driver's seat to face Moretti. 'We owe it to Charlotte Harrington and her family, Nick. They need answers as to why their daughter died and I intend to provide those answers if this is the last murder investigation I lead. You're either with me or you can get out now. The choice is yours. I will respect whatever decision you make. I give you my word. I value you, Nick. I'm not going to take you down a path you don't wish to tread,' she said.

Moretti bounced his head on the back of the headrest. 'You know I won't leave you to go it alone, that's unfair. Pip, you can see as well as I can that our subject is involved in a dangerous game that we, as mere murder detectives, aren't meant to pursue. Commander Allen is making that very clear. He'll know we've released the staff at Heath Hall by now, won't he? This is over, Pip. Call this off. We can brief our DCI and let him take the helm as the boat sinks,' he said.

Nash pressed the button on the internal door locks, and they clicked to open. 'Follow on foot and let me know if they get into another vehicle,' she said.

Moretti pressed the button again and the doors locked. 'Nice try, you're not tipping me out on foot to never be seen again. I'm not falling for that one. We've both made a career out of making choices, Pip. Some have gone well, others not so. Better to try than die not trying. Let's go,' he said.

'Welcome back, Maverick,' she said as she turned on the engine and activated the headlights.

Nash's phone blinked and the name "Allen" flashed on screen. Nash pressed cancel.

'Let's bring the investigation home,' she said.

'Yes, ma'am,' Moretti said.

Moretti exited their car, confident that Nash wasn't going to fly solo. He caught up with their subject within a safe distance so they wouldn't suspect they were being followed. The subject was walking downhill towards the main drag of Hampstead. The parcel they'd been given was tucked into their coat, held against their side by their arm. They continued past the parade of shops until they were near the junction where the old Hampstead police station was. They continued down a residential street until they were outside a semi-detached house. Moretti dropped back as their subject opened a gate to the house's front garden. A light came on under a small porch. Moretti heard the low bark of a dog before the subject entered the property, closing the door behind them.

Moretti phoned Nash. 'Subject's entered a property off Rosslyn Hill. They had a key,' he said.

'Let's get the team in,' she said.

Moretti phoned Sagona, instructing him to get their team on standby and passed the details of the address. Nash joined Moretti, parking up nearby, keeping the premises under observation. They'd keep the front door in view at the very least. She hoped they'd done enough and that their subject would remain at the address until the team was close by.

CHAPTER THIRTY-SEVEN

Sagona did his job well and the team were dotted around the subject's address awaiting Nash's call to arms. She'd had a message from Allen that said he was pleased she'd taken his advice and shut Heath Hall down. She hadn't replied. Let him believe that was the case, when in fact, it was as she'd left it. Jonesy had contacted her to say Petrov was preparing to leave and only one staff member had chosen to leave before him. The remaining staff were still there but would be gone soon.

Nash checked her watch noting the time in her decision log under the entry "Second Arrest Decision". 'Are we ready, Nick?' she said.

'Ready as we'll ever be,' he said.

They exited the car and approached the front door to the property. As they did so the overhead sensor lights illuminated the porch. This time there was no sound of a dog. Moretti lifted a flap to a letter box and was met by a gust of wind.

'Target's done one out the back,' he said.

Nash watched as Moretti stood back and booted the front door. He was joined by one of their detectives who pushed him aside and slammed the enforcer into the doorframe, caving the door inwards. Nash and Moretti ran through the house and out into a garden. They were faced with an open gate that led to the rear of other residential properties that backed onto an alleyway. Overhead, the thump of a helicopter's blades sounded in the air before the gardens became floodlit. The detectives were quickly joined by uniform officers, one of whom spoke with Moretti.

'We've had a call to suspects in a back garden; typical, it's a blue on blue,' the officer said.

'Maybe not. Keep searching and let's see what we turn up,' he said.

The officer shrugged and relayed the message to the helicopter, call sign India 99. It wasn't long before the observer in India 99 piped up over the radio. They'd got a possible suspect three gardens down in a bush. There was a dog in the garden barking and an open rear gate that accessed the garden was wide open. Nash and Moretti joined the foot race of officers towards where the helicopter was hovering. The officers were joined by a resident.

'Can you get your dog in, please,' a uniform officer said, loud enough to be heard over the din of the helicopter.

'I don't own a dog,' the resident bellowed.

Moretti moved towards the bush the dog was bouncing and barking around. He took hold of the dog's collar and handed the animal to another officer.

'Come out, the game's up,' Moretti said.

The bush moved and as the subject emerged, they were grabbed by Moretti.

'We must stop meeting among the bushes,' Moretti said, taking hold of the person's arm and placing his handcuffs on their wrists, behind their back.

'Very droll, Sergeant,' Middleton replied.

CHAPTER THIRTY-EIGHT

With Middleton in a police cell at Holborn, Moretti and Nash returned to Hendon where they intended to plan an interview. A search of her property was unfulfilling. In much the same way as Harrington's flat, it revealed little to the detectives. The parcel she'd been passed was missing, or at least if it was opened, they could find no trace of the packaging let alone what could have been inside. The exhibits of use they had were the passports in different names, both with Middleton's face, discovered in Harrington's flat along with the money, phones, and scanner.

Nash was up against the clock to establish a motive and method for Middleton to be charged with the murder of Harrington. Carter and Allen would be quick to see this quashed and Nash knew it. She'd acted within the law and that's what mattered to her. While she was in custody, Middleton's Labrador was placed with the pet service she employed when she was working.

Moretti pinched two Styrofoam coffee cups together at the rims and joined Nash in the briefing room. She was busying herself with a mind map on a blank murder board the inside team had erected for the inquiry. She turned as Moretti approached. He handed her a coffee and they both stood back to view what she'd created. In the centre was a photo of Middleton. Black lines of marker pen fired off from the picture. Some connected to form a framework, others didn't.

Nash spoke first. 'Who was Middleton trying to frame for Harrington's murder and why? Petrov finds the body with his belt around Harrington's neck. They'd both been out that evening and returned together. We learn from Dr King that it wasn't his belt that killed her. We find the lead in McNeil's van with our victim's DNA on it and a hair that matches the dark hair found on Harrington's skin. A dog's hair that's not from McNeil's spaniel and at present is of unknown origin. Then there's the ketamine. We know McNeil supplied the drug but who administered it and when? We think it was put in the steak, but there are several people who had access to it and could be implicated in that.'

Nash paused before continuing, 'Middleton told us she'd discovered McNeil's van in the basement car park. This is how she knew he was on site but she had somehow neglected to tell us. That's doubtful. She's meticulous in her organising and is having an affair with him. She arranged all his work. She must have known he was there. She could have easily taken the lead, at any time, and planted it in his van. She was close enough to McNeil to have the keys to access it or get a set cut if she'd planned Harrington's death in advance, which to my mind is the case here. This isn't a murder that was enacted in a fit of rage. It was premeditated. We can see there's been planning, with the drugs and from the way the scene was staged, to confuse us.'

She moved around the room before returning to Moretti who voiced his own take on the evidence.

'We know Middleton has access to Petrov's suite as I saw her changing his towels,' he said. 'She could easily have accessed his belt when he was out with Harrington. She was too open about being responsible for wiping the CCTV and keycode door data. An early bluff to appear open and honest the moment we arrived. *If* she's working with Carter's mob, then she's going to have knowledge way superior to ours. It's not going to be simple to prove. At best what we have, yet again, is circumstantial. We need motive and that's looking to be shrouded in secrecy. Carter and Allen will soon hear of her arrest if they haven't already.'

'You're right. I know she's requested a solicitor and if we work on the premise she's also working for Carter, then she'll say nothing in interview. There's a mole in Heath Hall that Carter is looking to catch and he's using the wrong traps. Either Petrov, Harrington or Middleton are playing for both sides. We can't be sure Harrington is the mole despite her death. The games these people play are all smoke and mirrors. I can't see my own reflection because of the smog. We deduced Middleton would bolt once the stable door was open. She ran to her handler at the first opportunity, fearing compromise and needing reassurance. We need to know what was in that parcel and where it is,' Nash said.

Moretti wagged his finger. 'Both Harrington and Middleton must have been using Harrington's flat. Middleton wouldn't leave those passports, and the other items, in a place she couldn't access in a hurry. The scanner fits with her "expert" knowledge of the room we used at Heath Hall,' he said.

Nash's shoulders slumped. 'A room we thought was clear of listening devices using the scanner Middleton provided. She was listening all the time. We'll need to get that scanner checked. I doubt it works in the way it should,' Nash said.

'So, Alex Petrov must be working for MI6 and is not under recruitment?' Moretti said.

'We know Carter went out of his way to meet him. A bold move, especially with all the press outside Heath Hall. He must be important to them. It doesn't explain why Harrington died. It explains why Middleton arranged for the image of Harrington and Maxim to be cropped. Middleton must have been told by Carter to sort that out as she knew the club owners. Maxim Petrov was a regular and she'd make all arrangements. The less Harrington's image was seen the better all round, for Petrov senior and MI6. We will never know for certain why Harrington was killed, but for what it's worth, I think she'd been sent to get close to Alex Petrov. She'd do whatever it took to keep close even if that meant entertaining Maxim at clubs. Petrov joked he thought she was a spy. I think she got too close to establishing who was the double agent and my money's on Middleton not Petrov. We will never prove it, Nick. Not without a confession or solid evidence. I believe Middleton killed Harrington, but I don't know where. We haven't established that and it's beginning to look weaker by the moment. I think we could charge Middleton with murder, but we won't win at court. Too many holes and not enough filler,' Nash said.

Nash and Moretti were interrupted by the sound of many feet marching along the corridor. It wasn't the sound of footfall they recognised. Commander Allen was the first through the door followed by a troop of plain-clothed officers. Nash stood. Moretti moved alongside her.

'This incident room is to remain untouched, Inspector. You're suspended from duty along with DS Moretti. These officers are from the professional standards pro-active team, and they will be dealing with the investigation from here. Running a confidential operation without my approval and in flagrant disregard of my instructions will not be tolerated. I had a call from Alex Petrov's solicitor. He is in discussion with the Foreign Office hoping to diffuse a potential political crisis. He asked me to pass on a message to you, personally, from Alex Petrov, "The scales of justice always favour the righteous." Apt in this case. I believe he is correct. You're a disgrace to the service, both of you. You may leave. Here's the card of the Senior Investigating Officer for this case, she'll be in touch.' With that Allen nodded at a dark-suited woman who stood behind him and exited the room.

Nash waited for a beat and approached the person she knew was the new SIO. 'Good luck, you know how to get hold of me,' she said, as both she and Moretti left the room.

CHAPTER THIRTY-NINE

Nash and Moretti sat in Nash's car. Both were staring back at the change of scene happening on the second floor of their incident room. Strange faces flitted past windows. It was as though they'd arrived for their first day at a new unit. A unit they hadn't asked for. Nash looked away to see her team milling around their own cars. She got out and Moretti followed her.

As she approached, they gathered round her.

'I want you to know you've been the best people I've had the privilege of working with,' she said. 'Commander Allen wants my head on a plate, not yours. I will do all I can to ensure your careers remain unsullied. Go home, rest, and await further instruction about where you are to go next. My bet is that they will bring you back here within forty-eight hours, once they've gathered all they need from this inquiry. DS Moretti and I won't be joining you. When, or if, we'll return is out of our hands. I have one more message before we leave.'

Nash paused. A flush of pain seared through her chest, and she felt the rise of tears. She inhaled deeply and let out a long exhale regulating her nervous system. Her inner strength returned, her shoulders set back as her spine straightened.

'Never let the bastards grind you down,' she said.

A round of applause echoed around the parade square. Nash beamed with pride at the seasoned faces before her. At the window to her office, the SIO, who'd been showing interest in the scene below, disappeared. Nash nodded to Moretti, and they returned to her car.

'Home?' Moretti said, clicking the passenger seat belt.

'Heath Hall,' Nash said, finishing a text message to Jonesy. She sent the message and spun their car around heading for the exit barrier to the car park.

* * *

On their arrival at the main gates to Heath Hall, camera flashes lit up the interior of their car and the faces of various media organisations leaned in, desperate to see who was in the vehicle. They could hear shouts of, "Is it true you are both suspended from the investigation?"

The detectives remained stoic as they faced the gates. Once the gates had withdrawn enough for their car to get through, she drove over into the drive and the gates closed.

'Fuck me, that news travelled quick,' Moretti said.

'That's professional standards for you,' Nash said.

She made use of the basement car park and entered Heath Hall via the lower level. JJ and Jonesy had remained there awaiting their arrival. Heath Hall was unusually quiet. The staff had left, along with Petrov and his team. Nash brought her detectives through to the meeting room. The two DCs had done a good job of removing all she and

Moretti had brought and the room was restored to its original purpose.

'Petrov left you this,' Jonesy said, handing Nash a swipe card.

'Can't believe it's ended this way,' JJ said, looking to Nash.

Nash gave a flicker of a smile. 'We're not done,' she said, waving the card in their faces.

'Why do we need to search the safe room?' JJ said.

'Because it's the one room we haven't searched and to see if this card is heavy enough to tip the scales of justice,' she said.

JJ scratched his head.

'Follow me,' Nash said, leading her small band of detectives who dutifully fell in line as they followed her up to the floor of the safe room.

Nash placed the card against the entry pad on the wall and the door clicked open. 'After you,' she said to her squad.

They walked into the main living area and Nash went over to the picture by Vladimir Kush. She put some gloves on and picked it off the wall. Taped behind the picture was a flash card. She photographed the card in-situ, on her phone, and removed the card from the picture.

Moretti watched as Nash dropped it into an evidence bag. 'I'll be damned,' he said. 'I doubted your confidence the picture would reveal anything. How on earth did you know that was there?'

'I didn't. Petrov's message, via our illustrious Commander, was enough to tell me it was worth visiting now he was gone,' she said.

She was about to seal it in an evidence bag when Moretti placed his hand on hers.

'Before you seal it, we need to view what's on it,' he said. 'I'm assuming Petrov's paranoia over personal safety meant he had a covert recording system here that only he knew about. My bet is our evidence is on that disc. This way, there'll be four witnesses who viewed whatever's recorded. If it goes missing once you book it in, we can give statements of what we viewed.'

Nash looked at her DS and the two DCs. 'If we view it, and it corrupts, the case will never see court. If I hand it over to the new SIO and let the tech guys image it, we'll stand a better chance of conviction,' she said.

Moretti laughed. 'You and I both know where this case is headed, Pip. Word is already out that we are suspended. The lead investigator and their DS in a high-profile murder case thrown off the inquiry. Professional standards being brought in is designed to imply incompetence or corruption. The smear campaign has already begun; smoke and mirrors fully in effect. If I'm to become a scapegoat for a political cover-up then I'll be damned if I don't go down fighting,' Moretti said, the two DCs nodding in agreement.

Nash tore the protective layer off the seal to the bag and closed it over. 'We do this the right way. I'm no longer the SIO, Nick. Let the new one make the decision. Let's get this back to Hendon and hand it over. All of you can witness that.'

CHAPTER FORTY

Nash sat at her kitchen table nursing a cup of tea. Two weeks had passed since she'd stepped away from Hendon after handing over the memory card to the Professional Standards SIO. The SIO had accepted the card with some trepidation in front of Nash's detectives. After completing statements of continuity for the exhibit, they departed. Nash's doorbell pinged. She got up and went over to the camera screen that showed the front door to the main house. She buzzed it open. Opening the door to her flat, she returned to the kitchen and sat back at the table.

The door to her flat closed and she waited for her visitor to enter. Commander Allen walked into the kitchen and pointed at a chair. Nash twitched her head, and he sat down, removing a pair of brown leather gloves.

'I'm out of tea and coffee,' Nash said, taking a sip from her mug.

Allen pursed his lips. 'I had one on the way over,' he said.

'To what do I owe the pleasure of this visit?' Nash said.

Allen leaned on the table. 'I came to tell you that the disc you handed over from the safe room was incendiary. Not literally, of course. It contained footage of Harrington collapsing and being strangled by Middleton using a dog lead in the safe room. The SIO is minded that Middleton intercepted the steak before it reached Petrov, took it up to the safe room and drugged it. Petrov never ate it. After Petrov retired for the night, worse for wear, she invited Harrington up. Harrington ate the steak, became drowsy and Middleton killed her. She bundled Harrington out and got McNeil to help her. He wasn't there when she was murdered. It's possible he intended to supply the drug to one of Petrov's men, like he said, but Middleton grabbed it for her own purposes. He's seen arriving in the safe room after. He colluded in covering up the crime,' he said.

'I heard they're both on bail,' she said.

Allen coughed. 'They were both bailed. McNeil is back in custody.'

'And Middleton?' Nash said.

Allen looked away. 'She's outstanding, whereabouts unknown,' he said, sheepishly.

Nash got up and walked to her kitchen window looking out over a communal garden. 'So McNeil takes the fall?' Nash said.

'Not at all, there's a warrant out for Middleton's arrest,' Allen said.

'Under what name? We both know she's an agent for the state. I bet the parcel I saw Carter hand her contained a new identity, passport, driving licence – you know, enough documentation to disappear without trace,' Nash said.

Allen picked up his gloves as he stood in preparation to leave. He hesitated. Nash sensed he wanted to get something off his chest.

'Harrington was suspected of being a double agent. Carter is as much to blame as Middleton for the murder, but proving it is another matter. Framing Petrov was ideal as he could never be prosecuted. As for McNeil, he was an ignorant pawn in a brutal game of espionage. It's left a bitter taste, Pippa.'

'How do you know this?'

'Carter met me near The Yard. All cloak and dagger, I was very uncomfortable with it. Middleton was feeding him information about your investigation. Carter didn't want you discovering the truth. I was left with one option – remove your squad. Professional Standards seemed the best choice to me. It appeased Carter and his organisation too. I had to do something; I had no choice.'

'Are we done?' Nash said.

'I came to tell you, I'm replacing your current DCI and I think you'd be ideal to take on the unit,' he said.

Nash turned from her window and walked over to Allen who raised his chin as she got closer.

'I wouldn't work for you for all the promotions in the world. Do what you will with me. I'm on suspension, or had you forgotten that?' she said.

'I'm pleased to say the initial findings of the professional standards team are that you led the Petrov inquiry in an exemplary way. The SIO requested that you be considered for a commendation. I have to say I wholeheartedly agr–'

'Please leave,' Nash said, interrupting him.

Allen looked at the floor and back at Nash. 'Look, I know I haven't been as supportive as I could. I was under extreme pressure and didn't know which way to turn. I'm here as peacemaker, not an adversary. We're on the same team,' he said.

Nash uncurled her fingers that had subconsciously balled into a fist by her side. She walked to a sideboard and brought out a plain white envelope addressed to Allen.

'While you are here, you can take this. I'll hand my warrant card in once my leave is completed. I have many outstanding rest days owed so don't expect to see me anytime soon. You know where the door is, Commander,' she said.

Allen took the envelope. 'Don't be too hasty, Pippa. Please. The service needs people like you. I hope you reconsider. I'll keep this for a fortnight before I submit it,' he said, as he left her flat.

Nash waited until he was away from her premises before she picked up her phone and called Moretti.

* * *

'I never thought you'd resign?' Moretti said, handing Nash a bottle of beer.

She'd elected to come to him. It was a good choice after Allen had tainted the ambience of her home. The evening was warm; a light breeze refreshed her skin as she sat on the roof deck of Moretti's houseboat and drank, both detectives at ease in the other's company.

'What will you do?' Moretti said.

Nash shrugged. 'I don't know. Travel for a bit, then I'll see how I feel,' she said.

'I wonder if they'll find Middleton,' Moretti said.

Nash sighed. 'I think the person we knew as Middleton is long gone, Nick. Allen told me Middleton was on the disc behind the picture. She killed Harrington in the safe room, McNeil helped get her out and in the water no doubt. Oh, I heard from Yvonne. The dark hair was from Middleton's Labrador. The beauty of Locard's principle in action, eh?' she said. 'And you, Maverick? What will you do next? You're free to return to work by all accounts. Wait until you're told, officially, of course. The weather's improving though, so I wouldn't rush.'

Moretti slugged his beer and set the spent bottle down on the deck. 'I don't know, Pip. Your news has come as a shock if I'm honest. I knew you were having thoughts of a move, but to hear you've jacked it in before your thirty years are up is unsettling to me,' he said.

'You'll adjust. We all do. I may change my mind after a break. Allen's given me a fortnight before he hands my resignation letter in,' she said.

'We could travel together, hunt for Middleton,' Moretti said.

'I've seen the way you live, Nick, I'd rather pass,' she said, smiling.

'Fair enough. Anyway, Middleton has my number if she wants to hand herself in,' Moretti said, laughing.

'Oh, she had both our numbers from the start,' Nash said, winking at Moretti.

The End

If you enjoyed this book, please let others know by leaving a quick review on Amazon. Also, if you spot anything untoward in the paperback, get in touch. We strive for the best quality and appreciate reader feedback.

editor@thebookfolks.com

ALSO IN THIS SERIES

LATENT DAMAGE (book 1)

When a respected member of the community is murdered, it is not the kind of knife crime London detectives DI Nash and DS Moretti are used to dealing with. Someone has an agenda and it is rotten to the core. But catching this killer will take all of their police skills and more.

COVER BLOWN (book 2)

A London advertising executive is found dead in her bath. Soon another woman is killed in similar circumstances. DI Nash and DS Moretti are hunting a killer, but finding a link between the victims is the only lead. What is it about their social media accounts that makes them a target?

SHOTS FIRED (book 3)

After going cold, a London murder case suddenly reignites when the weapon used is connected to murders in Glasgow and Belfast. DI Nash and DC Moretti investigate but come under criticism. Nash will have to go out on a limb but will Moretti defend her?

OTHER TITLES OF INTEREST

THE PERFUME KILLER by Linda Hagan

Stumped in a multiple murder investigation, with the only clue being a perfume bottle top left at a crime scene, DCI Gawn Girvin must wait for a serial killer to make a wrong move. Unless she puts herself in the firing line.

IMPURITY by Ray Clark

A seasonal worker is killed using a lethal drug unknown to forensics. He won't be the last. Can DI Gardener stop this spree, or is the killer saving his biggest murder till last?

www.thebookfolks.com

Printed in Great Britain
by Amazon